ALEATHA ROMIG

NEW YORK TIMES BESTSELLING AUTHOR

Book #3 of the SIN series
Aleatha Romig

New York Times, Wall Street Journal, and USA Today
bestselling author of the Consequences series, Infidelity
series, Sparrow trilogies: Web of Sin, Tangled Web, Web
of Desire, and Dangerous Web, and the Devil's
Series Duet

resemblance to any actual persons, living or dead, events, or locales is entirely coincidental.

ALEATHA ROMIG

"Lust is a tool, desire a trap. Wield the first, and you can take someone's soul. Fall into the second, and they can take yours."

~ Riley Shane

GOLD LUST

SYNOPSIS

Sexy, mysterious, with secrets hiding in the darkest of shadows, Donovan Sherman has stopped at nothing to achieve success. No one was immune.

One snowy night, his world and his life changed when he found Julia McGrath at the side of the road.

Finders keepers.

With Julia's happiness as his new goal, he must keep his past hidden. Unfortunately, the casualties he's left in his wake are back to threaten what he never thought he'd have.

Will Donovan's past sins destroy their future?

Can Julia navigate the unfamiliar landscape where lust is more precious than gold?

From New York Times bestselling author Aleatha Romig comes a brand-new age-gap,

family saga, chance meeting, contemporary romantic-suspense novel in the world of high finance, where success is sweet and revenge is sweeter.

Have you been Aleatha'd?

*GOLD LUST, a full-length novel, is book three of the Sin Series that began with RED SIN, continued with GREEN ENVY and GOLD LUST, and will conclude with BLACK KNIGHT.

PROLOGUE

The end of *GREEN ENVY*

Van

I watched as Julia walked away with one of the bodyguards, pausing to send me a sexy smile over her shoulder. It was a grin I could never tire of seeing. Eyeing the bodyguard, I nodded. I'd seen him around throughout the week. I could trust him—it's what I told myself as I answered the call.

Hitting the green button on the phone, I connected the private detective's call. "What do you have for me?"

"He's in Chicago."

"Phillip?"

"Yes, sir. He was slippery about it. Three days ago, his bank account received an interesting deposit. It didn't feel right. I started digging. The shell company is layered in shell companies. Today, the transaction came up."

"What transaction?" Hurry the fuck up was what I wanted to say.

"Airline ticket. Seems that your twin has been in Chicago since yesterday."

"He's not my twin; he's my triplet." Only Phillip and I are identical. Wrong word. We look alike. Olivia escaped that hell, coming out with blond hair. All three of us shared the same fucking green eyes as our bitch of a mother.

"Fuck," I mumbled. "Fuck him, we're leaving the city in the next hour." I looked over the crowd. Michael's car was out front, but I didn't see Julia. "Where in Chicago is he?"

"I found footage of him meeting with a man yesterday at a restaurant west of the city. I'll send you the picture from the security camera."

My phone pinged.

I tried to keep my voice low. It wasn't easy as the concoction of anxiety and rage was growing, a cauldron, bubbling to the surface. "Where in Chicago? I need a fucking pinpoint location."

"I-I'm working on it. I can't find hotel reservations under his name or any tied to his credit cards. That's why I didn't call sooner. I wanted to give you more. I'm sorry, Mr. Sherman, I thought you'd want to know that he's where you are."

I do.

Shit.

I ran my hand over my face. "Find him and keep him tailed until Ms. McGrath and I are out of the city."

"Yes, sir."

After hanging up, I saw a text message from an unknown number.

Ms. McGrath forgot her purse. I'm escorting her to the suite and back to the car.

I exhaled as I checked the attachment the private detective sent. "Fuck, it was a grainy picture of Phillip and Logan Butler." I would bet my company that Logan was the provider of Phillip's recent income, maybe the reservations were under his name. "What do you two have planned?"

Shaking my head, I sent my hypothesis to the private eye and made my way toward the front door.

"Mr. Sherman," the bodyguard said, his eyes wide as we passed in the rotating door.

I stepped out onto the sidewalk, and he soon followed. "Sir, how are you here?"

My heart thudded against my chest as I looked around. "Where is Ms. McGrath?"

"Sir, you were here. I saw you."

My circulation sped as I stepped forward, reaching for the man's collar. "Where is my fiancée?"

"She left."

"What the fuck did you say?"

"Mr. Sherman, she left with you."

Chapter 01

Van

My grip of the man's collar tightened, twisting as his face reddened and his eyes bulged wider. He was easily six inches taller and fifty pounds heavier, yet I didn't falter. "Say that again."

The bodyguard's voice came between gasps of air, small puffs of condensation rising between us. "Sir, I took her to the waiting car." His complexion continued to morph from ashen to a ruddy shade of red as he coughed and stiffened. "You were there."

"Michael's car is right there," I said, pointing toward the sedan with my free hand as Michael now came my way. "What fucking car did you take her to?"

"You were in it. I'm sorry..." He reached for my hand. "Please. I thought it was you."

The normal commotion around us faded into my rage-induced fury.

It was as if a lever had been pushed, changing everything.

The life I knew was now only visible through the reflection of a carnival mirror, one that distorted reality, making things appear differently than they existed. What had been right only minutes before was transformed into wrong. The world had turned upside down, and yet we were standing, my heart pounding and my pulse racing.

With my attention zeroed in on this man sputtering before me, I didn't notice the growing number of eyes upon us.

Footsteps hammered the pavement behind me seconds before a hand landed upon my shoulder. "Mr. Sherman."

"Don't fucking touch me," I growled under my breath.

"Sir." His voice came close to my ear. "It's me, Michael."

My neck craned as my gaze darted from the bodyguard, the man I'd trusted with Julia, to Michael. "He works for you?"

"Yes, sir. Albert has been with us for years."

Releasing Albert's collar, I shoved him away. "He's done," I proclaimed. "Fired."

Albert gasped for breath as he worked to maintain his balance.

"Where is Ms. McGrath?" Michael asked, keeping his voice calm.

"I-I thought it was your car," Albert said. "I-I saw Mr. Sherman."

This was my fault.

Fuck.

I vowed to protect her.

It didn't seem to matter what goal I set—women I loved always ended up getting hurt.

"What is he saying?" Michael asked.

My eyes closed and my nostrils flared as I took stock of this situation.

I should have told the security team about Phillip.

Fuck, I should have told Julia more, told both her and the security team that Phillip may appear as me. I ran my hand over my face as every muscle, tendon, and cell within me wanted to strike out, to hit, to pound, to ruin.

Opening my eyes, my gaze met Michael's. An unaccustomed emotion—fear— infiltrated my thoughts as I steadied my voice. "It was my brother. Who Albert saw —he's my brother. We appear physically identical."

We weren't identical in too many ways to count. Now wasn't the time to discuss the dissimilarities. Now was the time to find his ass before he hurt Julia.

"Fuck," Michael murmured as he turned and pulled his phone from his coat. Before making a call, Michael spoke in a low voice, "Sir, I'm sure we can find her. Let's go inside the hotel or get in my car. People are starting to record us."

Fuck.

"I'm not going anywhere but to Julia." As my voice continued in a low growl, beyond my erupting bubble of anger, I now saw the cell phones pointing our direction and heard the hushed whispers. "Make them stop," I said through clenched teeth as I lowered my face.

"I can't. If I do, it'll be worse."

"Worse? My fucking fiancée is gone." I pulled out my phone, ready to hit Julia's number.

"Mr. Sherman, unless you want to see your face all over the news media, please, come with me."

Keeping my eyes downcast, I pivoted toward Michael's car. Before we took a step, I turned back to the idiot who handed Julia over to Phillip. "You're coming with us."

The man's pale lips formed a straight line as he nodded.

"We need to hear exactly what happened," Michael added in a reassuring tone.

With Michael in the lead, I followed, trailed by Albert.

Michael opened the back door to his sedan for me. Taking a deep breath, I ignored the onlookers, ducked my head, and sat in the confined space. As Michael closed the door, deafening the world beyond the car, I lifted my phone, wanting a message from Julia.

Something.

Anything.

A fucking crumb.

Nothing.

Finding Julia's cell number, I hit call.

The silence was thunderous as Michael and Albert joined me in the car, and I waited for the call to connect. The city was filled with signals as some cell tower finally connected. Holding my breath, I listened as Julia's phone rang through mine.

Fucking answer, I screamed in my own head.

Her voice was a stab to my heart. "You have reached—"

Disconnecting the call and ignoring Michael and Albert's conversation, I tried the call again. The result was exactly the same—two rings and voicemail. I longed to listen to her voice, the tone and melody, forever. That was my plan. I disconnected without leaving a message.

"Mr. Sherman," Albert began from the front seat.

I lifted my hand. "I don't want apologies. I want Ms. McGrath."

"He looked like you," Albert said.

I nodded.

"Sir," Michael said, "are you now telling us that you have a twin."

Explaining my cohabitants within a uterus wasn't high on my priority list at the moment. "He's not a fucking doppelgänger. Yes, as I said, my brother and I are identical."

"And you didn't think that was valuable information for us to know?"

"I never thought..." he'd have the nerve, the resolve, or the determination to get this close.

My words and thoughts trailed away as the hotel's entrance caught my attention. I turned back to Michael. "The Waldorf has to have security cameras.

Can you get surveillance footage of this entrance? How about a license plate?"

"I'm working on that, sir. My company is already talking with the Waldorf's security team." His gaze met mine. "Now that we know you have a twin..."

"That information wouldn't have fucking mattered if Julia had been taken to the right car with the right damn driver."

My heart leapt as my telephone vibrated.

Please be Julia.

Disappointment washed through me at the sight of my assistant's name. Sighing, I hit the icon.

Andrew called from the airport. Is there a delay?

I replied:

Julia is missing. Contact Sherman and Madison PR. If any videos appear with me as the subject, get them the fuck down. If anything regarding me or Julia hits social media or any news outlet, shut it down. I want everyone in that department watching every possible outlet. Twenty-four seven. If they see anything with Julia, notify me.

Connie replied immediately:

Sir?

I hit the call button. As soon as Connie answered, I began speaking. "Phillip has her."

"Oh no," she gasped. "He has Julia?" Connie's voice grew higher with each word. "I was afraid—"

Fear.

It wasn't an emotion I was used to having, and yet Connie wasn't alone. The depraved possibilities of Phillip's plans were eating away at my resolve. Revenge was a bitch I was used to courting not battling.

With Connie, I responded truthfully. "This is my fault. I underestimated him. I never imagined that he—"

"Mr. Sherman, you'll find her. What can I do to help?"

"Tell Andrew to delay the flight and to call if that loser has the fucking balls to show up at the airport as me."

"Would he do that?"

Though my gaze was set out the window, I was no longer seeing the entry to the Waldorf or the people. Instead, my thoughts were racing with the options of Phillip's next move. "No. It's too risky. I know it's Phillip who has her even if Julia doesn't. I don't think that he'd risk my plane. He'd take her somewhere where no one will know."

"Airlines?"

Fuck.

"Airlines, trains, fucking boats leaving the Chicago harbor," I replied. "I want Sherman and Madison's security detail on this and this alone." I peered forward. "The firm you hired in Chicago will be in contact with Leonard."

"Leonard is on vacation. Flora Brooks is currently overseeing security."

"Contact her and tell her to drop everything else."

"Mr. Sherman," Connie said, her voice brimming with her calm reassurance, "your fiancée will know that Phillip isn't you."

"I never told her that I have an identical triplet."

Fuck.

That was on me.

"That won't matter. A woman knows the man she loves."

My thoughts went to a scene from nearly fifteen years ago. Madison knew that Phillip and I were identical, and yet she didn't know it was me—or that I wasn't him—at least not at first. With all the tools I'd tried to provide to Julia, knowledge on how to succeed at Wade, I'd failed to give her the basic information she needed now.

I wanted to believe what Connie said. "I hope you're right...before it's too late."

"Mr. Sherman," Michael said. "We have a partial license plate number."

"Run it." I spoke into the phone. "Call Ms. Brooks. Give her the number of the man I had trace your phone. Put all our teams together. I don't give a fuck what it costs. They need to hack into every damn public and private transportation option leaving from Chicago."

"I'm on it."

As I disconnected the call with Connie, Michael answered regarding the license plate, "We're running it. The last number is obscured. It will take time."

"I can't just sit here," I said.

"Mr. Sherman, where do you want to go?"

I wanted to go to the airport with Julia at my side. I wanted more of her—more, bigger, and better. I wanted what suddenly had an unobtainable price tag. I wanted what all the money or gold couldn't buy.

Closing my eyes, I tried to think of who else could help. As I opened my eyes, I said, "Fuck, take me to Wade Pharmaceutical's executive offices."

I searched for the number Connie gave me yesterday afternoon. It wasn't on my call log. I'd fucking called from a disposable phone. My text to Connie was quick, telling her I wanted Phillip's number again.

The number appeared on my screen.

I spoke to the front-seat passengers. "I have Julia's and Phillip's cell numbers. Can your company track them?"

"If their phones are on."

I rattled off both numbers to Michael. Once I was done saying them, I entered Phillip's number into my phone and hit the call button.

You want to fucking make a deal with the devil, I'm your man.

I was the only one to hear my comment as I waited.

As it had with Julia's number, the call to Phillip went straight to voicemail. Gritting my teeth, I contemplated leaving a message. Nothing I could or would say would matter. My call from my phone was enough to alert him that I was on to him.

Michael spoke to me in the rearview mirror. "Mr. Sherman, remember the man we sent to the McGrath home to collect her belongings?"

I hadn't. Now I did. "Yes."

"He just called. They sent him away without anything."

What the fuck?

As the car pulled away from the hotel, I called Gregg McGrath.

Chapter 02

Julia
A few minutes earlier

The bodyguard and I stepped outside to the waiting black sedan. When we approached the car, he opened the door to the back seat and peered inside. "Mr. Sherman, sorry for the delay." Taking a step back, my chaperone held the door open for me.

I entered the car, my senses filling with the scent of Van's cologne.

"Hi," I grinned as I settled onto the seat beside Van. "I tried to leave my purse."

"Julia."

There was a quality to his voice that sounded odd. "Is something wrong? Does it have to do with your call?" As I asked the question, the car moved away from the curb and onto the street. It was then I noticed the driver's reflection in the rearview mirror. "What happened to Michael?"

Van laid his gloved hand over mine. "I've decided to change our plans."

"Change our plans? I thought we were finally headed home."

His green orbs flittered from me to the rearview mirror and back as the fingers of his left hand tapped repeatedly upon the door's armrest.

"Van, talk to me. What's wrong? You seem..." I was unsure how to finish that sentence.

Off was a possible word.

His chest beneath his wool coat widened as he inhaled. The strumming of the armrest ended as he reached for my left hand, his attention momentarily on the engagement ring. By the time his gaze met mine, his expression had softened. "Marry me."

"I've already said yes."

"No, Julia, marry me today. Here in Chicago."

"What about our plans?"

"Our plans are for you to be mine forever. A change in venue doesn't alter the outcome."

"What about Mrs. Mayhand?"

The curl in his lips disappeared. "Why would you be concerned about her?" Before I could respond, he went on, "Paula will understand. This isn't about keeping my employees happy."

His employees. He called her by her first name.

A cold chill settled over me as I questioned, "Paula?"

"Yes, Mrs. Mayhand's name is Paula."

It was.

My skin prickled as I retrieved my hand from his grasp. Before I could ask another question or even address the uneasiness circulating through my blood-stream, I caught sight of the world beyond the windows. "We aren't headed to the airport."

"I told you, we have a change of plans."

"Van, what's the matter? Does this have to do with Wade?"

Instead of answering, Van changed the subject. "Tell me about your purse."

"I took it out of my satchel and left it in the suite." I lifted the handbag from my lap. "I have it now."

"Do you have your phone?"

"Yes."

"Turn it off. This day is about us."

I sat taller, still holding my purse. "What was your call about?" As I questioned, Van laid his hand over my purse.

"My rules. You're about to be my wife."

My stomach twisted. "Your rules?" Van had never previously used that phrase away from intimacy. His gaze seemed to harden with each passing second. "Is everything okay?"

In place of answering, Van turned his gloved large hand palm up. "Don't make me ask again."

Sitting taller, my skin felt tight and prickly as if Van and I were on the verge of a quarrel I didn't understand. It didn't help that we weren't alone. My gaze fluttered to the rearview mirror. I directed my question to the driver. "Do you work with Michael?"

From what I could see, this driver appeared nothing

like Michael or the large man who had accompanied me to the hotel room for my purse. Despite wearing a similar suit, his eyes were covered by dark glasses, and he had a thick beard.

"Do you work with Michael?" I asked again.

It was Van who answered. "Toby came from the same company. Michael had an emergency."

As my heart thumped within my chest, I opened my purse and pulled out my phone. I wasn't certain when I'd done it, but my phone was on silent. The missed call icon glowed from the bottom of the screen. "I-I missed two calls."

"They're from me."

Swiping the screen, I saw Van's name and exhaled. When I turned back, his hand was still extended. "Why did you call me?"

"I was worried when you weren't to the car yet."

"The bodyguard said he texted you."

Van forced a grin. "What can I say? I'm impatient when it comes to you."

Holding tightly to my phone, I tried to make heads or tails out of the recent development. There wasn't anyone I wanted to call, no one I wanted to be with other than the man at my side. Wanting my full attention wasn't unusual for Van. Perhaps I was letting my mind play tricks after all the warnings he'd given me.

"Trust me, Julia."

Exhaling, I nodded. Trust was the one thing Van had asked for most. I had no reason not to give it. I laid the phone in the palm of his hand. Beyond the windows, I saw the neighborhood I recognized. "Are we going to my parents'?"

Taking my phone, Van depressed the button on the side, turning it off. Next, he unbuttoned his wool coat and slipped my phone into the inside pocket of his suit coat. Once his task was complete, he finally answered, "It's a surprise."

My nose scrunched. "What surprise? I want to go to *our* home."

"We will. First, we have an appointment with a judge."

I shook my head. "This wasn't the way we planned our wedding."

"Something you may want to understand is that in all things, I have the final word." As I sucked in a breath, Van laid his hand over mine. "Oh, Julia, I want to hear your thoughts. I'll listen. But you need to trust that I know best."

"What is best about this?" I asked.

"I know that if we wed without your family and friends, you'll regret it for the rest of your life. I don't want that. You may not realize it now, but one day you will, and you'll be happy we made this change to our plans."

"We were going to marry in front of friends, your friends."

Van shook his head. "Your mother is expecting us, and Victoria is also waiting."

Victoria?

She'd told Van to call her Vicki.

"No, I don't want this." I spoke to the man in the front seat. "Please take us to Mr. Sherman's plane. It's waiting."

It was difficult to see the driver's expression with his dark glasses. Nevertheless, it appeared my demands didn't matter. The almost imperceptible shaking of Van's head overruled my request, telling the driver to stay the course.

Before I could protest further, the driver turned the car down the street that led to my childhood home. The houses were the same. The snow-dusted yards and landscaping with the pristinely cleaned sidewalks were as they'd been my entire life. This was where I'd grown up, and yet instead of seeing Van's new plan with the excitement of a new bride, I was racked with an unsettling sense of dread.

"What about Paula and Bruce?" I asked.

"Do you now believe in ghosts?"

Admittedly, my mention of Paula's deceased husband was a test. Something felt off with Van, and I couldn't put my finger on it. "No ghosts. I meant Jonathon."

"They'll watch our home while we're away."

The car turned into my parents' driveway.

"Away?"

"Yes, Julia, you deserve a honeymoon, one better than Skylar had planned for you."

The car came to a stop.

Toby stepped around the sedan on his way to my door. At the same time, the front doors to my childhood home opened as Arnold stepped out onto the top step. I turned back to Van.

"Van, I—"

My words disappeared as his lips met mine.

Hard and possessive.

His palms framed my cheeks as he held our kiss in place. For the first time since I'd met this man, I felt nothing.

No desire.

No heat.

No lust.

Nothing.

Not one of those emotions bubbled within me.

It was more than that. It was the absence of nothing.

There was a gaping void, a black hole of emotion that I couldn't identify. Everything about our kiss was as it'd been, and still it wasn't. A cold gust entered the car as the door to my side opened.

"Ms. McGrath."

In my mind, the sound hadn't been the opening of a door but a chink, a clank, the reverberating sound of breaking glass. As the frigid air swirled around us, splinters of glass landed in all directions.

Our snow globe.

Red sin.

Shattered.

Slipping away.

When Van pulled away, instead of desire, darkness swirled in his green stare, obscuring the golden flecks I'd come to love. His deep voice was resolute. "Julia, you're mine and we're going to make it legal today."

"Van—" His gloved finger came to my lips.

"One day, you'll thank me for this. You'll see what a mistake you were about to make and how I saved you."

"I don't understand what you're saying."

"You will."

"Take me home," I demanded one more time.

He lifted his chin toward the house. "This has been your home." He nodded. "Go. Your mother and Victoria are waiting."

What is happening?

As I lowered my boots to the concrete driveway, my skin prickled with uneasiness coursing through me. I tried to make sense of what had occurred, but it made no sense.

In the time it took to get my purse from our suite and for Van to take a call, the world had fallen from its axis. Nothing was as it was before.

Step by step, I forced myself to make my way across the driveway and up the steps.

"Ms. McGrath," Arnold said with a smile. "You're making your mother very happy."

I nodded before turning back, peering over my shoulder at Van. He was out of the car and speaking with the driver. His dark mane blew in the breeze as his coat hung from his wide shoulders.

This sensation I was experiencing was simply cold feet, I told myself. Perhaps it was the impending nuptials. I'd cancelled one wedding. It was understandable that I felt uneasy to marry so quickly.

"Ms. McGrath?"

I turned back to Arnold. "Mr. Sherman will be following me. You remember my fiancé."

"Yes, miss. A good man, no matter what your mother says."

A smile flitted over my lips as I reached out and squeezed Arnold's hand.

Something was eating at me.

One more look back at Van and that something hit me. Beneath his long wool coat, his suit pants, pleated to perfection, hung to the tops of his shiny leather loafers.

Calling from the archway, I asked, "Why did you change clothes?"

Van's quizzical gaze turned to me.

"Your clothes?" I repeated. "Why did you change and when?"

"Julia, we're about to be wed. The perfect attire is appropriate."

Since when did Van worry about the perfect attire.

Hell, I would be content to marry him in his mountain-man clothes, in our cabin, surrounded by snow.

Those thoughts were pushed away as my mother came hurriedly my direction.

"Julia," she gushed as I entered the foyer. "This is quite the about-face from yesterday. I couldn't believe when Mr...when Donovan called. I was shocked."

Chapter 03

Julia

*I*n the center of the foyer with people coming and going around us, I stood my ground, recalling the encouragement Van had given me to voice my opinion. "I'm shocked too, Mom."

Her arms opened wide as she offered me a reassuring embrace. Instead of stepping into her hug, my jaw clenched as I took a step back. "This wasn't our plan. When did Van call you?"

"It was earlier this morning. Your father and I immediately left Wade and hurried home. As you can imagine, it's been a mad dash to get things organized. Thankfully" —she gestured toward the tall, slender decorated tree— "the staff was able to bring back out a few of the decorations. I know it's not much and the holidays are over, but I think the white lights will do nicely. We can consider this a winter theme. The florist is due any minute with beautiful large arrangements with pine and white roses."

"Stop."

Mom went on as if I hadn't spoken. "Rosemary is

coordinating everything down here. There wasn't much selection from the caterer, but for a midday wedding, I think it will be acceptable."

Inhaling, I turned a circle, wondering if I should run out the front door to Van or perhaps out the back.

"By the time you come back down the stairs," Mom said, "the banister will be wound with more white lights." Her smile grew. "Perfect for your and your father's descent. Oh, and we have chairs being set up in the rear sitting room."

My head shook with disbelief. "Don't do this. I didn't want a big wedding. I don't want lights or chairs."

"The tent was removed a few days ago, but the rear sitting room will easily hold a hundred chairs."

A hundred?

My hands began to tremble. "Mom, I mean it. Stop. Stop all of it."

"Julia, you can't expect people to stand and watch you take vows" —her gaze narrowed as she took in my attire— "with you dressed like that." Her hand came to my hair. "Goodness, we need to get you upstairs. This will take longer than I imagined. Surely you had some plan of being presentable for your vows." She tsked as she pursed her lips. "I hope Donovan won't mind a delay. Look how pale you are. Oh, darling, I'll text Georgette and tell her it's an emergency."

Georgette was Mother's aesthetician. From what my mother had just said, if you paid well enough, Georgette was constantly on call.

Mom headed toward the front staircase. "Please, Julia, come upstairs. Let's have one wedding that isn't a farce."

My feet stayed resolute on the marble floor of the foyer. "I agree. I want a non-farcical, non-grand-production wedding. Van and I are leaving."

"You're what?"

"Leaving."

"No, not again," she said, her eyes narrowing.

As I was about to respond, the door behind me opened. Dad was the first to enter, followed by Van and finally, Marlin Butler. I watched for a sign from Van, one that he was unhappy with Marlin's presence. After all, he'd never hidden his animosity for the Butlers. I looked for the clenching of his jaw or the tightening muscles in his neck. There was no outward sign.

Either Van truly was a master at keeping his emotions in check or this was an alternate universe, and everyone knew it but me.

"Van," I said, taking a deep breath. "I was just telling Mom there's been a mistake, and we're leaving."

In two strides he was beside me. His long fingers wrapped around my wrist and his words were clipped. "Sometimes life throws curveballs. If you marry Donovan Sherman, you'll need to be able to handle them. Tell me you can handle this one."

If I marry Donovan Sherman?

Why is he speaking in third person?

Blinking, I stared up at his features. "Something is wrong. I want to speak to you privately."

His voice lowered. "We'll have plenty of private time on our honeymoon." After leaving a chaste kiss on my cheek, he stepped back.

Dad's smile was ear to ear. "Little girl, I don't care where you marry." He looked to Van and back. "I'm just so happy that Donovan convinced you to include us. My dream is to walk you down the aisle to a man you truly love."

Before I could respond, Mom reached for my hand. "Come, Julia. I've sent Georgette a text message." She turned toward the men. "The judge will be here at noon and the guests should begin arriving. Please, make yourselves at home. Gregg, be sure the caterers are prepared with finger foods and champagne as guests arrive."

Dad waved his hand. "Ana, Rosemary has it under control."

Mom's head shook. "We may be longer than I expected. We have a lot of work to do upstairs."

Before turning toward the staircase, I watched as Dad led Marlin and Van toward the back room, undoubtedly toward his well-stocked bar. As they disappeared through the archway, I decided that despite the hour being before noon, a drink wasn't a bad idea.

"I'll take some champagne," I said under my breath. As I followed Mom up the stairs, I added, "I don't need Georgette. If Van wants to marry here, I'll marry just as I am. He knew I wanted a small wedding."

"Oh, it will be small compared to what..." Her sentence trailed away before she regrouped. "On such short notice, it is a scramble, but I do believe we can get a nice crowd. As your dad said, Rosemary is calling our friends, but dear, understand, it isn't because it's you and another wedding. It's a workday and the timing..."

When we entered my bedroom, my feet stopped, my boots seemingly glued to the carpet. It wasn't the nearly empty shelves or the sensation that I was again Gregg and Ana's little girl. It was that lying upon my bed was my wedding gown, the one I'd chosen for my wedding to Skylar. The breakfast Van and I had delivered to the hotel room before checkout churned in my stomach. "No."

It was the only word I could think to form.

"Julia, I spoke with Donovan about it. He wanted to have a dress delivered, but well, this gown is perfectly good, it's altered to fit you, and we did spend..."

Lifting my hands to the side of my head, I pressed inward as I slowly spun around, taking in my childhood room and the items I'd chosen to leave behind. Upon the shelves there were books I'd loved as a child and pictures I'd decided not to take to Ashland. The drapes and bedspread were the ones I'd wanted when I entered high school. This was my room and yet at the moment, I felt like a traveler to a foreign country.

Perhaps it was that after packing many of my things yesterday, I never imagined being back in this room so soon. My mother's voice was speaking. I heard it in the distance, but I wasn't listening to her.

A dull buzz sounding within my ears had her and the rest of the world muted.

It was as if I were in an alternate reality.

Trapped.

Taking a deep breath, I stopped and lowered my hands. With one more look at the wedding dress lying on the bed, I reached for my mom's hands. "Mom, stop. I don't want this."

She stood, her neck straightening as her expression changed. Gone was the anticipation of a wedding or her need to make me presentable. The transition took milliseconds, yet I saw each and every one of the metaphoric wheels turning within her head. "Well, Julia, I'm glad you can finally admit it."

"Admit it? I've been saying it since I arrived. I don't want to get married today." I spun around. "Or here."

"Or to Mr. Sherman."

"No, Mom. I'm not saying that I don't want to marry Van. I'm saying not today and not here. This is rushed. It doesn't feel right."

She nodded. "Darling, you had a fling."

"He isn't a fling."

"Skylar confided in me that the two of you had never consummated your relationship."

My nose scrunched as my volume rose. "You spoke to Skylar about our sex life?"

"It was a commendable decision."

Pivoting, I took three steps toward the windows and pulling back the drapes, I stared down at the familiar street and frosted lawns.

Mom was behind me. "Julia, I respect and admire your decision to wait; however, have you considered that the lack of sexual fulfillment you associate with Skylar isn't his fault? He never was given the chance—"

I spun to face her. "Mom, stop."

Her face tilted. "Did you ever consider that he too felt unfulfilled? It's only natural for a man to seek—"

"Are you justifying his cheating?"

"Not justifying." She reached for my hands. "Equating would be a better word."

"Equating? Skylar and Beth to me and Van?"

"Julia, your lack of experience and satisfaction left you vulnerable to the enticement and seduction of a man like Mr. Sherman. He is older and experienced in ways..."

I freed my hands. "My relationship with Van is more than sex, and it's also none of your business."

She feigned a smile. "His assistance with Wade has been helpful. Your desire to suddenly help our company is also commendable. In the future, I hope you'll learn to draw the line at prostituting yourself."

My mouth opened as I tried to form words. Finally, they came. "What did you just say?"

"It's all right. It's all in the past. We can move forward from here."

I stepped toward the door. "This isn't happening."

"You took the opportunity to taste forbidden fruit. Skylar sowed his wild oats. Now the two of you can settle down, and we can rid ourselves of outsiders. Truly it will be better. Donovan has brought a spotlight on this family, one we neither want nor welcome."

"Oh my God," I spoke louder than I intended. "First you call me a whore, then you think I want to marry Skylar, and last you're dissing Van when he saved Wade's and your ass?"

"Julia Ann."

My fists came to my hips. "What part of that upset you?" Before she answered, I added, "Because the whole damn thing is upsetting to me."

Mom let out a long breath. "It's time for you to calm down. I've called him."

Taking a step back, I narrowed my gaze and asked, "Him?"

"Skylar."

"Why?"

"He's on his way."

"Again, Mom, why?"

Mom's voice sweetened. "Because, darling, it isn't too late."

"For me and Skylar? Mom, it's not only too late, it's done. I'm not sure I even like Skylar. I'm not sure I ever did. We were always just to be. I love Van."

"Your father can make a call. Your marriage license to Skylar was valid for thirty days. It hasn't expired yet. That means it's still valid."

A scream was on the tip of my tongue as my bedroom door opened and Vicki bounded inside with a garment bag over her arm and a smile across her face. "Julia, I can't believe you changed your mind and decided to get married here."

Chapter 04

Julia

"*V*icki," I said, opening my eyes wide at the sight of my friend.

Her smile dimmed as she closed the door behind her. It didn't take her long, barely only seconds, to see the distress my mother had either failed to recognize or found worthy of celebration.

"Ana," Vicki said, speaking to my mother, "Rosemary said not to tell you, but there's a problem downstairs."

Mom turned to my friend, her expression sober. "A problem?"

"Something about chairs and the caterer...I think she mentioned hot dogs."

"Hot dogs." Mom's voice rose two octaves.

Vicki shrugged. "Short notice. Availability. I'm not sure. I only overheard."

"Oh." Mom turned toward the door and back as she wrung her hands. "Julia. I'm going to go downstairs... Vicki, you'll stay with Julia, won't you? Georgette is on her way. Maybe if you could help Julia get out of" —she waved her hand up and down— "that." Mom pointed to the bed. "There's no reason not to use this perfectly good gown. It was altered for Julia, after all." She turned to me. "Do you want to shower and be fresh? It is your wedding day."

I didn't speak as I applied undue pressure to my already-gritted teeth. If I would have spoken, it would have been to ask which groom she wanted me fresh for. It was a conversation I wasn't prepared to continue.

Vicki waved her hand. "I'm sure it will be all right. There was also some talk about the number of mustard packets. Do you think it matters?" She shrugged. "Not everyone likes mustard."

Mom's eyes grew two sizes larger as her head shook. Mumbling under her breath, she left the room, closing the bedroom door behind her.

Exhaling, I relaxed my shoulders. "Oh my God, Vic. I love you."

Her voice sang out between laughs. "I figured if the hot dogs didn't send her into a tizzy, the mustard would."

"There's not a discussion on hot dogs or mustard downstairs, is there?"

"There will be when Ana gets there."

"Poor Rosemary," I said as I sat on the edge of the bed. "This is a clusterfuck."

Throwing the garment bag onto the bed, Vicki sat beside me. "Talk to me, Jules. What the hell is going on?"

"I don't know." I lay back and stared up at the ceiling. "I'm in an alternate universe."

"An alternate universe with super-sexy Van. I saw him downstairs."

I sat up and looked at Vicki. "Did he seem...the same?"

"I don't know what the same is. He looked fine in his suit. He was in your dad's bar with your dad, Skylar's dad, and his uncle."

Pushing off the bed, I stood. "Vicki, this isn't right. Van hates the Butlers. He wouldn't cozy up to one, much less two."

"Maybe he's just playing nice for the wedding before he goes all corporate apeshit on them."

"What do you know about Van's corporate anything?"

"I can read. While corporate intrigue isn't as fascinating as neuroscience, I did a little research after the New Year's Eve party."

There was never a doubt that out of the three of us —Vicki, Beth, and I—Vicki had the brains. That didn't mean Beth and I were lacking. It meant that Vicki stood out from the rest. She was on her way to follow in her mother's footsteps. Medical school and residency. Her next few years were mapped out in a direction she chose.

Vicki stood. "His history is impressive. No wonder everyone at Wade is scared to death. They know he could ruin them if he wanted."

I shook my head. "Again, tell me your source. Who said they're scared at Wade?"

Vicki's expression morphed. "It's not the best source."

My curiosity was piqued. "Tell me."

"Beth."

My lips opened, but no words came out.

"Beth is staying at the Butlers' house," Vicki explained.

"No shit."

"Oh man, it's been a shit show. Her parents are upset that she didn't come to them about the baby. Skylar's parents are upset that there is a baby. Skylar insisted she move in, and his mom has her tucked away in some back wing. If you asked her, it's dusty and hasn't seen visitors in decades."

I couldn't help but scoff. "That may be an exaggeration. Their house isn't that big."

"She's bored to tears, and when Beth is bored, she—"

"Talks," I said, finishing the sentence. "And she's hearing the Butlers' private discussions."

"According to her, they're freaked out about Van. They're concerned about what he'll do once he has control of your shares."

"He won't have control," I replied. "I will. Van's been supportive of me making my own decisions."

"What about a pre-nup?"

I shrugged. "Van has more money than my shares

are worth. He's already invested in Wade. I don't see a reason for a pre-nuptial agreement."

"How about so you can get some of what's his if things don't work out?"

Taking a step back, I shook my head. "Is this you talking or is it Beth? I'm not marrying Van with the intention of divorcing him and taking part of his money. I don't care about his money."

Vicki inhaled. "Girl, there are lots of rumors out there."

Spinning around, I inhaled and exhaled. When I faced Vicki again, I said, "I'm not getting married today. I'm not feeding into a frenzy or letting my mom turn this into a three-ring circus."

"I'm not sure about the circus, but there might be hot dogs," Vicki said with a smile.

"Do you know what Anastasia said?" I asked, using my mother's first name.

"I can only guess."

"No, I bet you can't. She said if I didn't want to marry Van today, Skylar would be here."

Vicki stood straighter. "Shit, that was exactly what Beth was worried about."

"I. Don't. Want. Skylar."

"I know that, and you know that. I'm pretty sure even Skylar knows that."

I turned to the wedding dress. "I'm not wearing that."

For the first time, Vicki seemed to notice the sparse

remaining items on the shelves. "You've packed your things?"

I nodded.

"Did you take all your clothes?"

"Not all."

Before I knew it, Vicki was in my closet.

I followed a step behind. "What are you...?"

Vicki turned with a grin, holding up a black gown I'd worn to a sorority dance. "I bet you're sexier than shit in this."

"I've never thought shit was sexy."

"Come on, you know what I mean."

I stepped toward her and ran the soft satin material through my fingertips. "I can't say that I've always dreamed of getting married in black."

"It's an interruption, to buy us time. From what you've told me about Van, he wouldn't pressure you into doing something you didn't want to do."

I wrapped my arms around my midsection. "I didn't think he would."

"You go freshen up as your mom said. Then convince Georgette you're wearing the black gown. I promise your mom will want to intervene. I'll get to Van and tell him to meet you up here. Say, in your old playroom. You two can work this out."

"My mom is calling people to be guests, and if I have my way, I'll be walking out on another wedding."

Vicki stood erect. "Honey, it's your wedding. You're the only person who should get her way."

"They'll think I'm a spoiled brat."

"Their opinions don't matter."

That brought a smile to my lips. "Van said the same thing."

Vicki held the dress against her chest and tilted her head. "Tell me what you wanted."

I bit my lower lip as I contemplated coming completely clean with my best friend. We didn't have time for the long version, so I spoke fast. "Van and I met when he found me along the road. I'd been driving..." Even with the abbreviated version, I filled Vicki in on more than I had in the past. When I got to the end, I added, "That's why I wanted to marry in the cabin. It's our special place. From our first encounter to the magical Christmas. Vicki, that's the man I fell in love with. Today, ever since he received a call, he's seemed different. I know, I'm crazy. I can see him. I can touch him, but it's all wrong. It's like someone else has taken over his body."

"Do you want to marry him?"

I looked down at the engagement ring on my finger. "I want to marry the man who rescued me in a snowstorm, the one who cut down a Christmas tree, who listens to me, who talks to me as if I'm not younger and inexperienced but as if I am capable of understanding, the one who explains things. I want to marry *that* man."

"Are you saying that you do want to marry him?"

"I'm not willing to marry him today. I want the

cabin." I took a deep breath and stepped back into the bedroom. "I'm a spoiled brat."

My friend was at my side. "You know what you want." Before I could respond, her smile grew. "And tell me why that's bad. If a man was in your shoes, they'd say he was determined or strong-willed. Because you're female, you're spoiled. I call BS." She reached for my shoulders. "What would Van do if he were determined?"

A smile curled my lips. "He'd convince me."

"Then convince him, Jules. Tell him the wedding is on but in Ashland."

Chapter 05

Van

Stepping off the elevator into the entry to Wade Pharmaceutical's executive office suite, I almost collided with Janie, Gregg McGrath's assistant. From her open heavy coat and the way she was shuffling through her purse, she seemed to be on her way out.

Before I had the opportunity to speak, she looked up, her gaze meeting mine as her eyes opened wide. "Mr. Sherman, why are you here?"

"I wanted to speak to Mr. McGrath. He isn't answering his calls."

Janie's lips curled. "Isn't it a little late to ask for Gregg's permission?" She closed her purse with a shake of her head. "He doesn't mind. He's too excited about today's wedding."

Her carefree words were a direct punch to my gut. "Today's wedding?"

She looked down at her watch. "We've closed the executive offices down and" —she waved her hand toward the empty room— "as you can see, most people are on their way to Gregg and Ana's home."

I repeated her last phrase—"on their way to Gregg and Ana's home"—letting the meaning sink in.

Fuck.

"You're saying that Julia and I are marrying today, here in Chicago at the McGrath home?" I asked, wanting confirmation.

"Why, yes." Janie took a step back. "Why do I feel like this is news to you?"

"Because, Janie, it is." I pulled my phone from my pocket and sent Michael a text message as well as one to the PI. He was supposed to tell me where to find Phillip. Instead, I was informing him. When I looked up, I asked, "Who announced the wedding?"

"Ana did, to the entire office, when she told Gregg that you'd called." Her expression turned quizzical. "It wasn't you?"

I shook my head. "No, it wasn't me. There won't be a wedding, but there may be a show." I hit the elevator button, summoning our means of escape from this building. Thankfully, it didn't take long before we were on our way down to the ground floor.

As we descended, I made a call to a connection I had at the Cook County Courthouse.

By the time I was back in the car with Michael and Albert, I'd confirmed a marriage license had been purchased this morning for Julia Ann McGrath and Donovan Sherman. The honorable Judge David Hill was en route to perform the nuptials.

"What the fuck is your endgame, brother?" I mumbled as I pressed the contact for the one person who may be in on this or at least had the possibility of being informed.

"Do you miss me that much?" Lena answered in lieu of a greeting.

"Are you still in Chicago?"

"No..." Her tone grew somber. "What's wrong? I hear it in your voice."

Gripping the phone tighter, I watched as Michael made his way through noon-day traffic toward the McGraths' home. "Phillip has Julia."

Lena's gasp could be heard through the phone.

"Does that mean you didn't know about his stunt?" I asked.

"I didn't. I would have told you. Where does he have her and how did you lose her?"

"I didn't lose her. He pretended to be me, and I don't know if she knows she's not with me."

"Va-an," Lena elongated the one syllable. "Please don't tell me that you were about to marry this girl and you hadn't told her about Phillip."

My lungs filled as I inhaled. "Telling her about Phillip would mean telling her about Madison and even Brooklyn. I was waiting for the right time."

There was no right time to tell Julia all the horrible things I'd done.

"I can call Logan and find out what he knows," Lena volunteered.

"He's in on it," I said. "I have a picture from a PI of Phillip with Logan taken here in the city yesterday. I also have it from a reliable source that a marriage license was purchased this morning under Julia's and my name."

"He can't marry her," Lena said. "Technically, he's still married."

My fingers of my free hand balled into a fist. "He wants to fuck with her."

"Van, I'm sorry. Maybe she's stronger than..." Lena didn't need to finish that sentence. She continued, "I'll do whatever you need. Phillip's my brother-in-law, but I won't stand back and watch the two of you ruin another woman's life. I should have done more the first time when I had the chance."

Lena's honesty was fucking brutal.

"I made mistakes. They're mine, not Julia's."

"Shit, Van. I told you to introduce us. Instead, you—"

Instead, I left Julia alone at the mercy of the consequence of my sins.

My voice lowered to a growl. "Now isn't the time for a lecture recounting my many faults."

"You're right about that." Lena paused. "You said a marriage license. What else do you know?"

"I know at least Logan Butler is helping. I know they're at Julia's parents' home and her parents think I want us to be married there today."

"This is insane. If he signs your name, aren't you the one married to Julia?"

My teeth clenched at the thought. "I don't fucking

want him near her. He'll hurt her." My mind was barraged with possible tactics—mental and emotional, as well as physical. If he touches her and she thinks it's me... "He will use this to screw with her and fuck me at the same time."

"Mr. Sherman," Albert turned toward the back seat.

"Hold on," I told Lena as I laid my hand over the microphone of the phone. "Did you find something?"

"Sir, the license plate is registered to a rental company."

I wasn't surprised.

"The name isn't Phillip's. It's a company. MMT."

MMT?

I spoke into the phone. "He's being financed. I think that's Logan or more of the Butlers."

"I can try to call Olivia," Lena offered. "She might know what's going on."

"What is his endgame? He can't be legally married to two people." I asked what I'd never thought I'd ask, "Could he have divorced Madison without your knowledge?"

I hadn't seen Madison in over ten years. She'd come to me for help, and I'd taken advantage of the situation. I'd done what I'd done my entire life, using my power and fortune to either get what I wanted or to destroy those who stood in my way. What I wanted was her, and with the knowledge that she was unobtainable, I'd gone to plan B.

Destroy.

"Could he divorce her?" Lena asked. "Yes. Would he? I don't think so. He has Madison's power of attorney. I only find out what he wants me to know or what Olivia tells me."

"Fuck, Lena. Call Madison."

There was a pause on the other end of the call. "I promised not to tell you."

"Tell me what?"

"I haven't told you because this went beyond you, Van. If you ask me, I blame Phillip equally if not more. He could have gotten her better care. God knows I offered to pay for it."

"What are you saying?"

"Madison has lost touch with reality. She hasn't been herself for a long time."

I tried to make sense of this news flash. "What do you mean? Everyone told me that she was in rehab and off-limits. I knew things went too far. I haven't tried to contact her."

"It wouldn't matter, Van. She doesn't remember anything concrete."

My heart sank. "She knows you?"

"No."

"Brooklyn?"

"No. Forget I told you this. It's not your fault. I doubt Phillip would divorce her, but in all honesty, they haven't been a couple since her last break."

My mind filled with memories of Madison.

The first time we met.

Her innocence and wonder.

She wasn't tainted the way Lena and I were.

She found delight in the simple things.

Reading, painting, and just life.

We'd been young. I was too young to recognize my obsession with her. Opening Madison up to my family had been the mistake. To her, Phillip was me without the pressure, the drive, or the fixation for more, bigger, and better. She saw what she wanted to see. I supposed she always had until reality stole her rose-colored glasses.

I'd accused Phillip of locking her up. He had. That wasn't on me.

I was guilty, but I didn't hold the key. He did.

My behavior may correlate to her fall. That didn't mean it was the lone cause.

No, that was my jealous brother.

All him.

His envy and lust for what I had.

My gut twisted as I applied Phillip's desire for revenge to his plans for Julia.

Something he'd said on this morning's call came back to me. 'You know what happens when you hit bottom? Absolutely nothing to stop me. Nothing.'

"He wants revenge," I said to Lena.

"It's more than that. He wants your life."

A succession of cars, much like on New Year's Eve, was lined up to enter the McGrath driveway. I spoke to Michael, "Is there a back entrance?"

My attention went back to Lena. "He can't have it. And he sure as hell can't have Julia."

"Do you want me to call Liv?"

Michael pulled the car up to a gate with a small box.

"No," I replied. "I'll let her know if I kill him." I disconnected our call without more explanation as Michael spoke into the box, saying something about catering supplies. My heart pounded in my chest as the gate moved and we drove onto a wide driveway that faced multiple garages with one door up a set of steps.

Not waiting for Michael or Albert, I hurriedly opened the door and rushed up the stairs as the door opened from within.

Chapter 06

Julia

Wearing one of my old robes from the closet, I sat before the large dressing table mirror in the bathroom attached to my bedroom. My hand fluttered near the pearl necklace I was now wearing. Vicki had brought it up, saying it was from Van. She promised to convince him to come upstairs.

As Georgette fretted and combed my long hair into silky waves, I told myself I was only acquiescing to give Vicki time downstairs with Van. Once she talked him into coming upstairs, we'd work this out.

"Darling, you need to condition more." Georgette's head shook. "These ends are..." She inhaled and exhaled. "Have you forgotten to use the products I gave you?"

She hadn't given anything to me. She'd sold my mother on the importance of overpriced shampoo, conditioner, spray treatment, heat treatment. The list went on and on.

"I've been out of town..."

At the sound of the doorknob, my gaze moved from

our reflection to the bathroom door. Hoping for Vicki, I was met with my mother's feigned smile. Her attention ultimately landed on the work Georgette had accomplished.

"She's so pale. Tell me that you brought makeup," Mother said.

Of course, she wasn't talking to me.

"Yes, once I get her hair styled, the makeup is next."

I gritted my teeth as the two women discussed my total disregard for hair care and the cinematic benefits of false eyelashes. It was when my mother mentioned that a photographer was about to enter the bathroom to record these moments for posterity that I lost what little reserve of decorum I'd managed to hold.

Pushing up from the bench, I shook my head, batting Georgette's hand away. "This is over."

Mom reached for my arm. "Julia, I need to speak to you about something." Her gaze met Georgette's. "In private."

Before I could say a word, Georgette slipped from the bathroom. Once the door closed, I crossed my arms over my chest. "I need to speak to Van."

"Skylar is outside. I realize this is a tricky situation. Marlin has spoken to Donovan and if you decide to marry Skylar—"

My pulse quickly sped up as my voice echoed off the tile of the bathroom. "Marlin told Donovan I wanted to marry Skylar?"

Mother's lips pursed as she shushed me.

Pushing my way past her, I opened the bathroom door. Staring my direction was a woman with a camera, her lens pointed at the wedding dress now lain out in a picturesque way upon the bed, and a man holding a large white screen.

"Ms. McGrath." The woman offered me her hand. "I'm Cindy, your photographer."

Taking her hand, I forced a smile. "Hi, Cindy. Please leave. This wedding is cancelled." I tilted my head toward my mother. "Talk to her about your compensation."

"Julia."

My mother's voice was lost as I bolted beyond my bedroom door, closing it behind me. At the end of the hallway was my first fiancé. "Go away, Skylar. This is a shit show and I'm leaving."

He offered me his hand. "Come on. I have my car parked behind your parents' garages."

His words stopped me in my tracks. "You're offering to help me?"

He took a step closer. "Our families are fucked. I can't figure out what's happening, but from what I've been able to gather, I'm supposed to step in at the last minute, a proverbial prince on a white horse."

A smile came to my face. "You've never ridden a horse."

"My dad and uncle have been overly secretive. Beth kept telling me that something big was planned." He shrugged. "I think she is right."

Great. I have Beth to thank for my escape.

When I didn't take Skylar's hand, he lowered his voice, opening the door to a nearby bedroom. "Hide in here."

My decision took less than a second as I heard the voices from my bedroom grow louder as the door down the hallway began to open.

Once inside, Skylar spoke in a whisper. "I know you think you love Mr. Sherman." My lips came together. "Jules, maybe you do. I'm the last person to comment on love. I'm my own shit show and I know it."

"I love the man I've gotten to know."

We both stilled, my heart racing, as voices passed by the door.

"You know, I've known Beth forever, but since she's moved in" —he shrugged— "I'm getting to know her differently. If that makes sense."

"I'm really glad, Skylar. I hope you two can make it work."

My breath caught in my chest at the sound of my mother's voice calling my name. As Skylar stepped toward the door, I shook my head and pleaded with my eyes. Using his head, he pointed to the other side of the door. Quietly, I hurried behind him milliseconds before he opened the door, obscuring me from Mom's view.

"Ana, are you ready for me?" he asked.

"Not yet. Um, did you see Julia?"

Afraid to breathe, I stood stock-still as Skylar explained he'd been waiting in the guest room the entire time and offered to help with the search. The smile I saw as he closed the door reminded me of the boy I knew when we were kids. There'd been no pressure for forever back then. We were just two friends.

Maybe we could be again.

I waited for the footsteps and voices to fade.

Slowly, I opened the door, only hearing the din from commotion below. Approaching my bedroom door that stood slightly ajar, I paused. The photographer's equipment was still present, yet there wasn't anyone within my suite.

Closing the door, I engaged the lock before stripping from the robe and quickly donning the same clothes from this morning. In the bathroom, my fingers worked the clasp on the string of pearls. Coiling the necklace in the palm of my hand, I debated its fate. There was nothing about them that appealed to me.

Why wouldn't Van bring them himself?

Why did he send them with Vicki?

While I couldn't comprehend what was happening, I knew without a doubt I didn't want to be a part of it. I also didn't need a reminder.

I couldn't think about Van, his intentions, or his thoughts regarding Marlin's declaration. The sledge-hammer continued to rain down on our snow globe, scattering the shards of glass to obliteration.

Holding back tears at the total decimation of my world, I left the pearls on the bathroom counter, pulled on my boots and coat, and grabbed my purse. Begging my own pulse to slow, I leaned against the bedroom door. As I turned the knob, I gasped.

Green eyes shining from a handsome face met mine.

Telling Van I was sorry but I wasn't going to marry him today or in this house was on the tip of my tongue. I'd anticipated the hardness in his tone from downstairs. I'd feared the lack of emotion from our kiss in the car. My mind swirled with the possibilities that all led to our demise, and yet...

Before any of that could happen, my world took another flip.

"Thank fuck." Van's deep voice sent a tremor to my tummy as his palms landed on my cheeks, pulling me toward him.

The principle of conservation of energy stated that the energy of two interacting bodies within a closed system remains constant. In the car, I didn't believe it. The energy between us was gone. However, applying the principle, perhaps it wasn't gone but in a resting state because here, within a millisecond, I knew the principle to be true.

The energy was back.

Much as magnets of polar opposites, we came together.

My body melted against Van's; my soft curves landed upon his hard planes. While he held me close, my arms went around his torso, wanting and needing to be within our own closed system.

My lips opened, welcoming Van's tongue as my heart beat in triple time.

I couldn't get enough as I pressed into his kiss with his heart pounding against mine.

When our kiss ended, my vision blurred as tears teetered upon my lower lids. "I don't understand what's happening," I admitted.

"Fuck." Van's one word played on repeat as he ran his fingers over my face and his hands down my arms and torso. As if I were a sculpture or a piece of art he needed to inspect, his touch was possessive and gentle at the same time. "Tell me that you're all right."

Nodding, I said, "I am now. Why were you acting—"

His finger landed on my lips. "Julia, I'm so sorry. I'll explain everything."

It was at that moment that reality returned.

Voices in the distance came into range accompanied by the calling of my name. It was my turn to lay a finger upon his strong, firm lips. "Not now, Van. We need to get out of here. Once we're gone, I want to know everything."

Van reached for my hand. "Are you sure you want to walk out on another wedding?"

I had never been more certain of anything in my life. "I'm sure."

As we came to the end of the hallway, the voices from down below became clearer. One voice I thought I recognized was ascending the grand staircase. Instead of calling my name, I recognized the low murmuring of curses. My eyes grew wide, knowing that the voice wasn't coming from the man at my side.

Van's grip of my hand tightened as his body stiffened. "Get behind me."

I couldn't describe what I didn't understand.

My mind couldn't comprehend what my heart knew without a doubt. "Please, Van." I wasn't even sure what I was asking. Somewhere deep in my soul, I knew I loved the man holding my hand. I knew our snow globe's best chance of survival was to get away. It was a lot to ask of a man like Van.

He met challenges head-on.

"Fight this battle another day." My plea was barely audible as I tugged him toward the back steps.

Donovan Sherman was a proud and stubborn man. The conflict within him was as evident as a flashing neon sign. There was a battle at hand that either I couldn't see or didn't want to recognize. Either way, for the first time in hours, I knew I was with the man I loved and who loved me.

"I don't run from a challenge." His response came through clenched teeth as tendons and cords came to life upon his stiffened neck.

With all that was happening, I had an odd realization.

It was the clothes he wore.

Van was dressed in the jeans, boots, and button-down shirt with a sports coat from earlier at the hotel. The suit, Italian loafers, and overpowering scent of cologne were gone. As if the pieces of a puzzle were finally snapping into place, I said, "There are two of you."

Chapter 07

Van

Two of me.

No.

There was one of me.

One Donovan Sherman.

One man with a record of unmatched success.

One man who held the lives of others in his hands.

Hands.

My gaze went to where Julia and I were connected, her petite hand encased in mine.

For the first time I could recall, my priorities shifted.

Yes, I wanted to confront Phillip, to watch my brother fall in disgrace, and to expose his sham to Julia and to the guests a floor below. Most of all, I longed for him to suffer for his sins as he had tried to make me suffer. My list didn't end with him. The Butlers were involved—I felt it in my soul. This wasn't only about hurting me and Julia; it involved Wade somehow.

My instinct was to get to the bottom of their plans, and above all, to prove once and for all I was superior.

No, there weren't two of me.

I'm the only Donovan Sherman.

And yet the light Julia brought into my life was once again beside me. The glow coming from her blue orbs as she stared up at me and pleaded to get away from here was as bright as the sun reflecting off a blanket of snow. Despite its blinding glare, I couldn't look away.

Julia encompassed the pinnacle of everything I desired.

She was the sun, and I was the snow.

Her warming effects tingled through my circulation. In the short time since I'd found her, I'd become hopelessly addicted. She was the culmination of everything I'd missed in my life. It wasn't about what she did or how she looked or sounded. It was deeper.

Simply, her presence calmed the monster within me.

In the hallway of the McGraths' home, I was at a precipice—face Phillip and expose this farce, our past, and our sins, or surrender to Julia's desire and flee with her at my side.

Taking a deep breath, I led Julia the opposite direction from the front staircase—away from Phillip.

I knew where we were going. It was the direction from which I'd entered the second floor, up the back stairs, the ones that she'd shown me on New Year's Eve. With raised voices above and below, Julia held tight to my hand as we hurried downward, toward the kitchen. Our boots clicked on the wood steps.

At the landing where the stairs turned, Julia stopped. Her expression grew more concerned as she looked down and back up. There wasn't another option. We'd be confronted either way. Reassuring her with a nod, I gestured for us to move toward the first floor.

The man at the bottom of the stairs with his back to us had worked for the McGraths for the better part of his life. Maybe that was why he'd chosen to believe me when he found me entering through the delivery entry. Possibly it was because of our first meeting. Or perhaps it was his adoration of Julia. There wasn't time to question.

I tugged on Julia's hand. "Come on. Arnold is on our side."

Her blue eyes opened as she gave into my lead.

Hearing our approach, Arnold acknowledged our presence with a nod before he began barking orders toward the kitchen staff and stepped away from the staircase. In doing so, he took everyone's attention with him. As our boots landed upon the first floor, we pivoted toward the hallway to the delivery exit.

A new obstacle stood in our way.

A stout woman with graying hair appeared.

Ready to confront her, I gripped Julia's hand. It was Julia who released my grasp and went forward. The woman's arms spread wide as she surrounded Julia in her embrace.

"I'll miss you, child."

"I'll miss you too, Rosemary. I'm sorry to leave you to deal with Mother and this mess."

The two women pulled apart as Rosemary's face blossomed and her smile grew. "After all these years, I've gotten good at cleaning up her messes."

Julia grinned. "Thank you."

"Now, hurry. Mr. Sherman's driver is waiting."

I offered the woman my hand. "Thank you, ma'am."

She shook my hand with the strength and confidence of a person in control. If I had ever questioned my regard for this woman, in that instant, I knew I liked her as much as I liked her husband.

"Mr. Sherman, you take care of our girl. That's all the thanks I need." A rosy blush came to her cheeks. "Arnold and I, we never had a child of our own." She glanced to where Julia's and my hands were again united. "We claim Miss Julia as ours. Tell me you'll make sure she's loved, safe, and through it all, you'll never hamper her opportunity to fly."

I couldn't have said it better.

My gaze met Julia's before turning to Rosemary. "I promise to do my best."

"Nothing more we can ask." She peered through the window of the delivery door. "Now you two scoot."

As Rosemary opened the back door, Julia leaned forward, leaving a kiss on Rosemary's cheek. "I love you."

"Love you too, child. Be happy."

Gray skies added to the chill as I wrapped my arm

around Julia, and we hurried across the driveway to Michael's car. This wasn't the time for formalities, and honestly, I wasn't a fan of people waiting on me anyway. I opened the door and ushered Julia into the back seat of the waiting car. As I slammed the door shut, closing off the outside world, I exhaled.

"To the airport?" Michael asked.

"Yes," Julia responded before I had the opportunity.

"Ms. McGrath," Albert said, speaking over the seat. "Ma'am, I'm sorry."

Julia shook her head. "I'm where I belong now. That's all that matters."

It wasn't, but I couldn't deny that since Julia disappeared with Phillip, both Michael and Albert had been working nonstop as a team to find her. Turning away from the men in the front seat, I soaked in the beauty of the woman again at my side.

My palm came to her soft cheek, pulling her face toward me. "I love you."

Inclining her face to my touch, her eyes momentarily closed. When the bright blue orbs were again focused on me, she said, "I feel it. I still feel it. Do you?"

"That I would search heaven and hell for you? That I'd face every devil or demigod to find you. Yes, I feel it to my bones."

"It's real, Van. Red Sin."

Is there another explanation for the way I feel?

An inexplicable attraction. "I'm never letting you go."

"It's not an option."

As Michael drove beyond the McGrath home and our car faded into Chicago traffic, Julia's smile dimmed. The relief at having her in my grasp lessened as the adrenaline in my system waned. "Did he hurt you?"

Julia sat taller as her brow furrowed. "Who is he? Your twin?"

I nodded. "It's more complicated than that, but yes. We're identical."

"No, you're not."

Our world was imploding around us—missteps, revenge, and plots—and in that one phrase, Julia righted everything. "You knew?"

"He...I...it felt wrong. You're not identical."

"We're not."

She reached for my hand, surrounding it with two of hers. "I knew something wasn't right. I couldn't understand. And yet somehow I knew."

"Did he hurt you?" I asked again.

"No, not physically. I was confused and afraid..." She looked down and turned toward the window. "You weren't listening to me." She turned back. "*He* wasn't." A tear slid down her cheek. "You always listen."

Reaching for her chin, I lifted her gaze to me. "I'm listening now. Whatever happened, I'm so sorry, Julia. I owe you more than an apology. I should have told you about Phillip. I underestimated him."

"Yes, you should have told me," she agreed. "I thought I was crazy."

"No, beautiful. You're the sanest person I know."

"I knew something was off, but my mind tried to make sense of what I saw." She exhaled. "You two may look alike, but that's where the similarities end."

"Did he touch you?" It took every ounce of self-control to keep my tone and question calm.

"He kissed me."

Do I want to hear more?

"Van, it was so odd. It felt wrong—like our connection was gone. I thought he was you, but he was cold. He insisted we marry today." She exhaled. "I thought you'd changed. Skylar said..."

When she didn't complete the sentence, I asked, "What did he say?"

She shook her head. "He helped me hide. Whatever was happening, I think Marlin and Logan were in on it."

"I promise, Julia, Phillip will pay for what he's done. They'll all pay."

"I'm not looking for revenge. I just want us back in our snow globe."

Julia didn't need to look for revenge. I had plenty for the two of us. My list didn't stop at Phillip. As she'd already said, the Butlers were in on this too. "Skylar helped you?" I asked.

A smile curled her beautiful lips. "For the first time in years, it felt like he and I were friends again. None of the pressure for love and forever that we both knew wasn't real." She swallowed. "He's not guilty. I mean, he is of other things, but in this debacle, Skylar was as confused as I was. He said he was supposed to save the day. My mom said my marriage license to him hadn't expired."

"Phillip was going to leave you at the altar?"

She held tight to my hands. "I don't know. He dismissed everything I said. I thought you no longer cared."

My palm gently cupped her cheek. "Never doubt my love, Julia. I'm many things. I've done horrible things and while I may deserve anything and everything that is thrown my way, you don't. You're going to learn about things that I'm not proud of." My thoughts went to the call with Lena. "I'm dealing with a new revelation right now."

"What?"

"More of the damage I caused." I shook my head. "I'd give away every dime I ever made to show you that I'm a changed man."

"Van, I don't want to change you."

"You don't know what you're saying."

"I do. I love you. I love the man who saved me, who has shown me physical love, and above all, the man who listens."

Her lips brushed mine.

"Our snow globe is waiting." I wrapped my arm around her, pulling her against me. Julia reached beneath my sport coat, holding onto my torso. With my chin on the top of her head, I inhaled scents of fruit and sunshine as my heart rate took on its first normal cadence since Julia slipped from my grasp.

Her stare turned my way as my phone vibrated.

"I don't want to let go of you," I admitted, wanting to ignore the world.

"I'm not going anywhere without you, Mr. Sherman."

Pulling the phone from my jacket pocket, I saw the icon, indicating there were eleven missed calls. The incoming call was from Connie. "I should take this."

Julia nodded as she sat up.

Beyond the windows of the sedan, the tall buildings were giving way as Michael took an entrance to I-90. As our speed increased, the heaviness of the city fell from my shoulders. I was never happy in the city and watching it disappear behind us was the relief I didn't know I needed.

"Connie," I said, answering her call.

"Mr. Sherman, thank God you answered."

The relief was short-lived. "What is it?"

"Andrew called. There are state police at the airport."

My body stiffened. "Why?"

"They want to search your plane."

"For what?"

"They won't say."

"Tell Andrew to wait until my legal team is informed."

"I took the liberty of calling Oscar Fields. He called

a firm in Chicago. They have a representative on their way to the airport."

"Tell Oscar to call me when he knows something." I spoke to Michael. "Change of plans."

Julia's eyes opened wide.

"We're driving to Ashland."

Chapter 08

Julia

Crossing the state line and entering Wisconsin, I had a flashback of driving the rental car into the unknown. At this point in the journey, I'd been concentrating on what I was leaving behind. Three weeks later, I wasn't leaving anything behind as much as I felt that I was going toward my true life, the one I wanted with my entire heart and soul.

Van and I had yet to discuss Phillip or anything else in much detail. One of the reasons for our lack of discussion was the men in the front seat. It was reassuring to see Michael and I now knew my bodyguard's name was Albert. In some way I'd grown accustomed to both of them. That said, Donovan Sherman was too private of a man for me to ask him with an audience present to explain how we'd come to this point.

As the landscape changed with each mile, I came up with more questions while at the same time settling into the peace that came in Van's presence. I wished I could explain this, even to myself. Within Van's orbit, the world calmed. The glass of our globe defied principles of matter, reversing its shattered state, growing stronger, and keeping us safe from outside forces.

After nearly two hours of listening to one-sided conversations, I knew that some of my perceptions of safety and isolation were contrived. To think we could simply put today's chain of events behind us and move forward was wishful thinking or the dream of a spoiled child, and yet when left in our bubble, the possibility felt real.

My thoughts wandered back to Lincoln Park.

How is my disappearance being handled?

Does anyone know that the man with them isn't Van?

If I had my phone, I would call Vicki and ask for details. I'd also tell her that I was safe and with the real Van. A small part of me worried about what was left of my reputation and wondered how many guests my mother had corralled for their second time to not see me marry.

I couldn't learn any of that.

I didn't have my phone. The last time I saw it, Van —a.k.a. Phillip—turned it off and placed it in the breast pocket of his suit coat. When I mentioned that to Van, he texted Connie and promised to have a new phone as soon as we arrived in Ashland.

In the time that had passed since Van's initial call with his assistant, he'd stayed busy talking with multiple people. When one call ended, he'd return numerous text messages and then begin a new conversation. It wasn't that he was keeping me out of the loop. I was present but with the benefit of hearing only half of everything.

Taking what I could from Van's side of the conversations, I'd been able to paste parts and pieces together.

"Mr. Sherman and Ms. McGrath," Michael said from the front seat. "We need to stop for gas. We're approaching Madison. Would you two like a minute to stretch your legs?"

"I would," I volunteered.

Van simply nodded as he ended his most recent phone call. "Are you hungry?" he asked as we passed a multitude of restaurants.

"You don't like public dining."

"Ashland is still five hours away. I could use a cup of coffee or a stiff drink." He looked to the men in the front seat. "Ms. McGrath and I are going to go to that diner next door. After the car is filled, join us for some food."

They both agreed.

Standing upon the concrete, I stretched my muscles as the cool Wisconsin air swirled around us. The sky above was filled with shades of gray, reminding me that we were headed away from the cold of Chicago to the frigid air of northern Wisconsin. And still, as Van reached for my hand, I couldn't come up with anyplace I'd rather be.

"Is my laptop in the trunk?" I asked. I'd been thinking about my recent research.

Van reached for my hand. "I believe it is. Or it was sent on to the plane."

We began walking through the parking lots toward the diner. The sign glowed in the waning sunlight. "What happened with the police at the plane?" Van had filled me in on that much.

"The lawyer demanded a search warrant."

"They didn't have one?" I asked, puzzled.

"They did, but it was for the wrong name."

"What name?"

"Julia Sherman."

I stopped in place. "They were searching for me?"

Van tugged me toward the restaurant. "It was a delay tactic."

"To keep us in Chicago?"

"To keep you from leaving without me. Wires were crossed." Before he could tell me more, the sound of customers and the aroma of food met us as we entered through the glass doors. "Two," Van said to the hostess.

"I'll be a minute," I said, taking a step toward the back of the restaurant.

Van held tight to my hand. "Wait for Albert."

"Is he going in the bathroom with me?"

"Humor me."

Exhaling, I walked with Van as the hostess led us to a booth near the front windows. When I sat, Van followed on my side. After the hostess took our drink orders and left the menus, I leaned into Van's side. "Will you talk to me while we have a few minutes?"

He nodded. "I won't be able to scratch the surface, but I'll try." He placed his arm over the top of the booth, turning my way.

"I have questions to ask."

The golden flecks that were missing in Phillip's eyes glistened under the harsh restaurant lighting. "Ask. But before you do, make me a promise."

"Anything."

"Don't leave me."

"Why would I leave you?"

Moving his arm, he laid his hand over mine. "I don't scare easily, Julia. Today I was terrified of what Phillip would do to you." Van exhaled. "I was terrified because I've been on the other side. I've hurt others to hurt him."

My gaze narrowed as a new revelation hit. "The picture of the couple in wedding clothes. That was Phillip?"

Van nodded.

"Why would you keep your brother's wedding picture up in your office? Especially, a brother you don't like." I watched as Van wrestled with himself. The battle was evident in his eyes, the way his body tensed, and his hesitation. It was a conflict he had to endure alone. No matter how much I wanted to help, I couldn't. Van hadn't offered me the knowledge or the weapons to fight alongside of him. Instead, I was merely an observer.

I turned my hand until our palms came together and

our fingers intertwined. "I won't leave, Van. Tell me who you hurt."

Before he could answer, Michael and Albert entered the restaurant, taking a table not far from us.

Van began to stand, undoubtedly offering me the bathroom break I'd been denied. I held tight to his hand. "Van, tell me first."

"Madison."

It was one word.

One name.

One dagger.

My question came out stronger than I felt, as if I hadn't been stabbed in the heart. "You hurt her?"

Van leaned back and exhaled. "This can't be explained over coffee and sandwiches. I won't lie to you. I haven't. What Madison and I shared was unhealthy at best. Obsessive would be a better description."

"She married Phillip?"

Van nodded.

"Why did you keep the picture?"

"Because the necklace she's wearing in the picture is one I gave her."

"I don't understand," I admitted. "She wore a necklace from you in her wedding to your brother."

The waitress set two cups of coffee on the table, bursting our bubble of isolation. "Have you made your decisions?"

We hadn't even looked at the menu.

I glanced around at the other diners. "I'm sorry. I haven't looked. Do you have chicken salad?"

The waitress nodded. "Yeah. Do you want a sandwich or salad? The salad comes with fruit."

"Salad."

Van lifted the menu and laid it back down. "Chicken sandwich and chips."

I busied myself with adding creamer to my coffee until the waitress was gone. Finally, I asked, "Why did you display the picture."

"Because I'm a sick fuck."

I laid my hand on his arm. "Van, I need answers. That isn't an answer."

"It is, Julia. I wasn't invited to the wedding for obvious reasons, but I went anyway. Minutes before the ceremony, I went into Madison's dressing room. I took the pearls she was wearing and gave her a diamond necklace. She thought I was Phillip, or at least at first she did."

My hand fluttered near my throat. "You...he sent pearls up to my bedroom. He gave them to Vicki to give to me."

Van's face fell forward, his chin dropping to his chest before straightening his shoulders and neck. "It was a message. I'm fucking glad he didn't deliver them himself."

"I was upset."

Van's green stare focused on me. "You were?"

"Yes, I didn't want to marry at my parents. I thought

if I could just talk to you alone and if you'd listen, we could stop the whole thing. Instead, you...who I thought was you...sent a gift via my friend."

"Where are the pearls?"

"I left them on the vanity counter in the bathroom."

Van's lips curled and his cheeks rose. "Because you were mad at me?"

"I thought I was." I nodded toward the opening on Van's other side. "I will take you up on your offer."

As Van stood, he said, "Albert will follow."

I reached for Van's hand. "I know he's following because of what's happening. Just know, I won't leave you, Van. I won't disappear through some bathroom window."

"Well, fuck. Now Michael needs to watch the windows from outside."

Lifting myself up on my tiptoes, I kissed Van's cheek. "Our conversation isn't done."

"Hurry back."

When I returned, Van was staring down at his phone with a scowl. He looked up as I approached.

"What is upsetting?"

Van stood, letting me scoot into the booth beside him. As I settled in, he handed me his phone. My mouth opened as I read the headline.

'Pharmaceutical heiress leaves Donovan Sherman at the altar. Wade Pharmaceutical stocks plummet.'

Chapter 09

Van

Nearly fifteen years ago

As the plane took flight, I laid my head against the seat, telling myself that Texas would forever be in my rearview mirror. Dusk filled the sky with clouds in shades of red and pink. While others may have seen the beauty, I saw it for what it was. The red was from within.

Red. Scarlet. Crimson. Fiery.

Associated with heat.

The color of blood.

The color of rage.

"Phillip didn't win." It was what I'd been telling myself since I walked away from Madison's dressing room. He couldn't.

How could he win against me?

In what world?

I'd won. I'd been the one to find Madison. She'd been mine first. I'd named my company after her. I'd found a slice of paradise for us to live in, to keep her...

With me, she'd have the world at her fingertips.

With him, she would live the life of our parents. A mundane existence of contrived norms.

"Mr. Sherman," the flight attendant asked, "would you like a drink?"

I blinked up at the attendant.

Thankfully, the plane was small, having a row of single stand-alone seats on one side of first-class. My only interruption would come from this smiling woman.

"We have sodas, water, wine..."

I'd had a drink, or four, at the airport bar. Still wearing the slacks and shirt from the cheap tuxedo, I looked like a real loser. I'd even had a few propositions from women willing to take my mind off my troubles.

My attire and demeanor appeared as though I'd been left at the altar.

I hadn't.

It was worse.

Madison had gone through with the wedding.

Fucking email.

After giving the flight attendant my order, I pulled my BlackBerry out of my pocket and opened the email from Liv. The message was short and to the point, letting me know the wedding went as planned. No one mentioned seeing me at the venue. She was even kind enough to attach a picture of the bride and groom.

I hit the attachment and waited.

Delivering my glass of bourbon, the attendant said, "I'm sorry, sir. You can't use that in flight."

The phone was in airplane mode. The picture was

saved to my internal file. Instead of telling her any of that, I dropped the phone into my breast pocket, lifted the glass of bourbon, swallowed the amber liquid in one gulp, and ordered another.

I didn't need the damn picture.

It was burned into my mind for all eternity.

For a moment, I imagined it was me standing with Madison, smiling at the camera. I could pretend we were surrounded by family wishing us well. No. Fuck, even my imagination wasn't that strong.

With the exception of Liv, the whole damn venue could go up in smoke, and I wouldn't lose a minute of sleep. After consideration, I added Lena to my list of attendees who would survive my mental massacre.

Isn't that the way it is with fantasies?

A person had the opportunity to think and rethink until they hit every marker.

With each rendition of the wedding in my head, my imagination became more morose. The flames started in the kitchen. No. Candles ignited the cheap décor, spreading quickly and blocking exits. Lena and Liv were talking in the hallway, discussing the mistake both Phillip and Madison had made. They'd come to the conclusion that I was the better groom when the structure exploded.

Another drink of the amber liquid.

My throat no longer felt the burn as the alcohol coated my throat and stomach.

Far below, lights identified towns and cities separated by large dark spaces. The red had tempered as the bourbon mixed with the onboard meal. It was as the captain announced our arrival in Appleton that I made my decision.

My family was dead to me.

With the exception of my sister, I was done.

Stick me with a fucking fork.

I was Donovan Sherman, and when I stripped off this cheap tuxedo, I'd set it ablaze like my fantasies of the venue. I had no intention on wasting another minute on anyone who shared my DNA. However, I vowed that at every opportunity I discovered to use my wealth or power to my advantage, I would.

My car was waiting in long-term parking. The worst part about living in the middle of nowhere was the lack of direct flights. With a four-hour drive to my house in Ashland, I made the right decision by staying the night at a hotel.

I'd give myself this one day and night.

When my eyes opened in the morning, I would move on.

It was the next morning when I woke that I searched the pockets of the tuxedo. Hell, if I didn't set it ablaze, I'd leave it in the trash. The shop could charge me for the damn thing. I didn't give a fuck.

As my fingers came into contact with Madison's pearls, I pulled them from the depth of the pocket. I contemplated leaving them for the maid, throwing them in the trash can, or igniting them with the tuxedo.

Do pearls melt?
Are they real?
Are they old?
A family tradition?
Sentimental?

At the front desk, I asked for a padded envelope. After scribbling Lena's address on the front, I dropped the pearls inside, sealed the flap, and paid the postage. With my good deed for the year complete, I washed my hands of my past.

"For better or worse, motherfuckers. I'm moving on."

Van
Present day

'*Pharmaceutical heiress leaves Donovan Sherman at the altar. Wade Pharmaceutical stocks plummet.*'

Julia stared at the screen of my phone. In actuality, the story was more headline than substance. Nevertheless, I was admittedly caught off guard by the change of events.

"Why would they purposely want to sabotage the value of Wade?" Julia asked.

"The million-dollar question is who are *they*?"

"Your brother and the Butlers," Julia replied without hesitation. "We were up in my bedroom and Vicki said you were in Dad's bar with Dad, Marlin, and Logan." Her head shook. "I knew something was up. I even told Vicki that you didn't like them and wouldn't cozy up. She said that maybe you were playing nice before sabotaging them."

"Vicki thinks I'll sabotage Wade?"

"She said she'd heard that the Butlers were worried about what you would do."

"So their solution was to bring in a fake me..." I mused aloud.

"But he isn't you. He can't pretend...can he?"

"He already did. The damage is done."

"Then undo it. Have Sherman and Madison make a counter statement. Call Connie."

I shook my head. "They've already obtained the shock factor. How many news stories do you read or see that later have a retraction?" I didn't pause. "The initial story sells news or gets hits. They've accomplished that. The retraction will get lost."

"There's nothing we can do?"

"I'm weighing our options."

"What options?" Julia asked. "They succeeded if they wanted to delay our return to Ashland and deflate the value of Wade stock."

"No, Julia. They didn't win. This is far from over. I also won't go to the press and feed their frenzy. Instead, we'll use their actions to our advantage."

Julia's face paled before me, the blush leaving her cheeks.

"What? Are you all right?" I reached for her arm. "Did he do something?"

"Van, what if my parents were in on this? Remember the letter I gave my mom from your legal department?"

I took a deep breath. "It warned against selling or purposely devaluing your stock."

"Do you think they were in on this?"

"You do know that we could sell all of our stock in Wade," I said, "both of us, and walk away. Your future is yours. It doesn't need to be tied to Wade." I wouldn't do that. I'd run Wade into the fucking ground to watch everyone who has hurt Julia suffer. Still, I wanted her to know she had the option of walking away.

"I know. It's what Mom said about me taking a pious position because of you." She grinned. "I love you, but not for your money or as a safety net, Van. Tell me honestly. I trust you. Is my determination to make Wade succeed a hopeless battle? Am I a spoiled brat who wants her way?"

"No, beautiful. You're not spoiled. You're determined."

Julia grinned. "Vicki said the same thing."

"Vicki is right and so am I. Your determination is something I love about you. Don't compromise it for the easy way out. Will we succeed? I can't promise. It would be fucking easier to sell Wade off for parts and watch the Butlers face the consequences of what they just pulled."

"Is that what you think we should do?"

Phillip had said that Julia was my replacement for Madison. Staring at her, seeing the shine in her blue eyes as she talked about her family's company, and listening to her resolve were all glistening examples of how Julia was different than Madison.

Madison wasn't a fighter.

She wanted complacency in her life.

It set her apart from Lena and others like us.

In hindsight, I thought I could make Madison's dreams come true. No, I thought I could change her dreams into mine, wanting more, bigger, and better. Julia was different from the moment we met.

It was Julia's grit that sent her walking in a blizzard. Her honesty and openness attracted me, but it was her self-assuredness when we parted ways for the first time that secured my interest, setting a hook to ensnare my heart.

"Be honest," Julia said.

"I am. I always will be. I want the Butlers to suffer. I've told you that our history goes way back. The jury is out on what your parents know. I don't give a fuck about them." Her smile dimmed. "That's the truth. My only concern is you. If you want to keep fighting this contest, I'll be your biggest supporter."

"I don't want you to throw good money after bad."

"Wade isn't publicly traded. The headline was more clickbait than accurate information."

"So the value of Wade hasn't plummeted?"

"It's a perceived value, affecting secondary indicators of worth, such as borrowing power, market share, and the willingness to invest. My people are working this, checking with the other investors."

"Those SPACs?"

I nodded. "We want to know what their stance is on this. Are they wanting to sell or buy?"

"How will you know?"

"I'll use some of my shares as bait. It's already in motion."

Julia's eyes opened wide. "If you sell…"

"I'm not selling. I'm testing the waters."

"But if the press finds out, it will look bad."

I couldn't help but smile at Julia's understanding. Each moment, she confirmed that she truly was born to oversee Wade. "Donovan Sherman isn't selling," I said. "Neither is Sherman and Madison. The shares are wrapped up in shell companies. No one will know their origin."

"I trust you."

"To figure out what motivated today's shit show, we need to go back to the beginning."

"How far back?"

A smile came to my lips. "A blizzard."

Julia's smile grew, sending sparkles to her eyes. "I'd love to go back to there."

"It's obviously the beginning of our relationship and my interest in Wade, but maybe for recent events, we only need to go to our engagement announcement. Phillip began calling my office following the announcement."

"And you never mentioned it."

I reached for her hand. "I underestimated him. I never imagined…"

"Tell me what you did about his calls."

"I had Rob, my PI—"

"The one who takes pictures of Brooklyn," Julia interjected.

I swallowed. Julia deserved to know the truth about Brooklyn too. It would take a lifetime for me to confess all my sins. Nodding, I went on. "The PI lost track of Phillip. I'd had him searching in Texas. All I knew for sure was that Brooklyn was staying with my sister."

"Olivia," Julia said.

"Yes. Yesterday, Connie told me that Phillip had called her private number."

"How did he get it?"

I shrugged. "I'd had enough. Calling Connie's private phone was a bridge too far. I called him."

"Yesterday?"

I picked up the cup of coffee, remembering our conversation. "Connie said that during his calls he'd become abrasive. She was worried about what he could do."

Julia sat against the window, turning my way. "He wasn't abrasive to me. He was...cold."

"Phillip told me that he wanted to meet you. He wanted what I'd taken from him."

"What did you take from him?"

"It seems almost everything. He said that there was nothing to stop him. And then this morning, Rob called. It was the call I got before we were to leave the hotel."

Julia's brow furrowed. "Interesting timing."

Fuck. It was. I hadn't thought of that. "It was when I learned Phillip was in Chicago."

"And then I was gone."

"He didn't win, Julia. You're with me. He'll never get to you. That's all that matters."

"What was their end game?" she asked. "If I'd gone ahead with the wedding and then he left me at the altar with Skylar coming in to save me...what would that have accomplished?"

"Getting me out of your life."

Julia sat back, her lips together as she stared out the window. "It would have."

"I'm sorry."

"No, don't be. He wasn't you." Her eyes widened. "Van, I need to call my father and Vicki. They need to know he isn't you, too."

"They should already know. Arnold was going to inform Gregg after we were gone."

"If they know, I don't understand the headline. I didn't leave you at the altar. I left him." She let out a long sigh.

Beyond the windows, darkness had fallen. We'd both eaten a portion of our meals. It seemed that neither of us had much of an appetite. "Let's get back in the car and I'll fill you in on how we've used this travel delay to our advantage."

When she turned toward me, her eyes were lighter. "Do you remember saying you wanted me to move into your bedroom?"

A smile lifted my cheeks. "I seem to recall you saying I was bossy."

"You can be."

"Is that a problem?"

"No. In most instances, it's intriguing. I like it."

I slid from the booth, and standing, I offered Julia my hand. "Come, let me explain what Jonathon has been up to in Ashland. And when we get home, I can't promise I'll let you sleep."

"Maybe I should take a nap in the car."

My hand went to the small of her back as we stepped to the front counter. After paying for our meals, the four of us headed to the parked car.

Chapter 11

Julia

My eyes fluttered open as the car came to a stop. As we began to move again, I sat up, wiped a bit of drool from my lips, and hoped that Van hadn't seen the drool in the darkness. The pitch-black sky beyond our windows was filled with millions of stars. "I love how pretty the sky is here."

"Did you have a nice nap?" Van asked with a grin.

"Tell me I didn't snore."

"Your secret is safe."

I peered up to the front seat. This whole bodyguard thing was new to me. Maybe Van made them sign some kind of 'do not disclose' form, stopping a tell-all book from surfacing about my snoring and drooling.

"We're almost home," he said.

"I like the sound of that."

A few minutes later, Michael brought the car to a stop at a large iron gate blocking the driveway to Van's property.

"This is new," I said.

"The gate was here," Van replied. "I guess I never

cared enough about what was on the property to close it." He lifted my hand, bringing my knuckles to his lips. "I care now."

"Is this part of what you were telling me, part of what Jonathon has been doing?"

Van nodded as Michael punched a code into a box. Once he was done, the gate effortlessly moved to the side, allowing us entry. The car took the winding driveway up and up until the golden glow of the house came into view.

Soon the car was parked on the wide driveway.

"The house is equipped with a new security system." Van pulled up an app on his phone. "With heat and motion sensors, we can see who is, or in this case who isn't, inside."

I let out a sigh. "I wish life were easier."

"Life is easy, beautiful. I'm determined to make it safe."

Standing on the driveway, frigid air turned our words into vapors. Pushing my hands deep into the pockets of my coat, I watched as the two men unloaded our luggage from the trunk. It was then that I recalled the items we'd sent ahead to the plane. "What about all of our things on the plane?"

"Andrew and Ruth landed hours ago. Everything has been delivered."

At the front door, there was a new keypad with a sensor.

"Tomorrow," Van said, "all the entries will be programmed with our handprints."

I shook my head. "I don't want to say you've gone overboard, but—"

Van pulled me close as he opened the door. "Nothing is overboard when it comes to your safety."

A sense of peace washed through me as we entered beyond the French doors. Warm lighting filled the large living room, giving a reflective quality to the large windows overlooking the bay. Besides the items that had been delivered from the plane, the room was exactly as it had been the first time I entered. That first time, the house seemed large, open, and foreign. After being away, it truly felt as if now I was home.

I'd been lost in my own thoughts and not paying attention. I looked up as Michael and Albert carried our belongings up to the second story.

Once they'd disappeared, I said, "It's late for them to drive back to Chicago."

"They aren't leaving."

I watched for their return. "Where are they going to stay?"

"Tonight, I offered to let them stay here. We have plenty of bedrooms. If they take my offer to work for us full time, they'll stay on the property."

"You offered both of them a job? Why did I think you'd be upset with Albert?"

Van's lips quirked. "I was...livid."

"Well, I guess that means he knows what he's in for

if he works for you." My gaze went back to the second-floor landing. "I like him. Michael too."

Van tugged the zipper of my coat, bringing my attention back to him. "I noticed. I also know you aren't comfortable with the whole security issue. I understand that having people around infringes on our privacy. Believe me, it's not easy for me either. My hope is that you'll be more comfortable with people you've already met."

"Are they interested in the job?"

"I made them a damn good offer."

I leaned closer to Van, pressing against him. "That's not to say that I'm not a bit disappointed we won't be alone."

"Oh, we'll be alone in our bedroom. They'll each stay in rooms in the south wing. Tomorrow, assuming they take the offer, they'll move to the guesthouse. Only one night of keeping our volume under control."

Kissing his lips, I stepped back and removed my coat, laying it on one of the chairs. "Where is the guest-house? I've never seen it."

"On our property."

"Our," I repeated with a grin. "I really do want to marry you."

"That's good because I want to marry you."

I turned toward the front doors and back. "I have a question that may be dumb."

Van too had taken off his coat. Laying it next to mine, he turned my way. "Questions are never dumb,

Julia. Questions are a search for knowledge. Why would smart devices be so popular if people didn't ask millions of questions a day?"

"I suppose you're right. I could just ask my phone—when I get one."

"Connie has your new one at the office. You'll have it tomorrow. What's your question?"

"You said you and Phillip are identical."

"We share the same genetic blueprint."

"Okay, I understand enough about genetics to know that identical twins come from the splitting of a fertilized egg. What about the sensor?"

"What about the sensor?"

"The one by the door. If it's set to recognize your handprint, won't it also recognize his?"

Van shook his head. "Interesting fact about identical twins, they don't have matching fingerprints. It's a myth or a fabrication of mystery writers and crime shows. We're also not genetically identical. We started with the same genetic material as one another, but as soon as the fertilized egg split, our cells wove their own strands of DNA and split into more cells. The difference is usually only about five percent of our makeup, but it's enough to prove we're not the same person."

"I didn't know any of that," I answered honestly.

"Well, my pursuit of that knowledge was fueled at a young age, primarily by my need for autonomy. You can say that I was happy with the findings." He gazed past me to the kitchen. "Are you hungry?"

I peered down at my watch. It was nearly ten at night. "A little."

"Let's look in the kitchen for something to eat, and I'll get us a bottle of wine to take upstairs."

As I followed a step behind him, we entered the kitchen. As I opened the refrigerator my mind stayed on our conversation. "Who is older?"

Van turned. "If I answer you, will you drop this subject until tomorrow?"

Basking in the refrigerator's illumination, I crossed my arms over my breasts. "My need to know increased significantly when I was ambushed slash kidnapped by a man who I didn't know looked like a man I do. Oh, and there's the part about him demanding to marry me and the theory he was going to break my heart in front of guests and allegedly send me running back to Skylar." I took a deep breath. "I think under the circumstances, I deserve answers."

"And our birth order will help how?"

My arms fell to my sides. "I don't know. I'm curious." I lifted the lids off a few dishes. "Oh, this looks like artichoke dip. Do we have crackers or bread?"

Van selected a bottle of wine from the rack and gathered two glasses. Before he answered any of my questions, the sound of the men's footsteps descending the staircase came into range.

"If you go up to our room," Van said, "we'll secure the house. I'll show them where they'll sleep, and I'll warm the dip and find something to go with it. Once I join you, I'll grant you three questions."

I lifted my eyebrows and closed the refrigerator. "You'll *grant* me? Is this like a wish thing?"

He came closer, lowering his timbre. "No, there's no limit on the number of wishes I'll grant or orgasms. Questions tonight are limited to three."

Attempting to swallow, I noticed that my mouth had suddenly gone dry. I lifted my chin, keeping Van in my sights. "You're doing that thing with your voice." And words, but honestly, he could be reciting the Declaration of Independence with his deliberately deep and sexy tone and my nipples would grow hard.

Van leaned down, purposely breathing warm gusts onto my neck and collarbone. His tone lowered another octave. "What thing?"

Closing my eyes, I shivered. When my eyes opened, my vision was filled with his emerald-green stare. I took a step back. "His eyes don't have your gold flecks."

Van's head tilted. "What?"

"Phillip's eyes. They don't have gold flecks like yours. I noticed it in the car when I first got in with him. I thought maybe you were mad about your call."

Van lowered his forehead to mine. "I'm sorry you even know he exists."

I lifted my hands to his broad shoulders. "Van, I want to know about *you*. Your twin is something about you. Your sister and your parents are about you."

He shook his head.

"It doesn't mean I want to meet them or see him again. I just want to know."

"Go upstairs. I want you to get to know me better."

My lips curled upward. "Is that possible?"

"We'll find out."

Letting go of his shoulders, I paused. "I've never been in your room."

"Never? Even when I wasn't home?"

"Never. I figured if you wanted me there, you'd say."

The kitchen filled with a pop as Van uncorked the wine. Adding a wine stopper, he handed me the bottle and glasses. "I want you there. You know where it is." His volume lowered. "I want you naked, on the bed, waiting for me."

My breathing hitched.

It was crazy what Van could do to me with only words. In three phrases, my core dampened and twisted. "Will I still get my questions?"

"Give me my wish and you'll get your questions."

Chapter

12

Julia

"It's only a room," I told myself as I turned left at the top of the stairs. To the right, Van was showing each man to his own room. I had a fleeting thought about what they would eat. After all, I had our wine and Van was bringing up a snack.

I had no idea how this would all work.

Would Paula be asked to cook more meals for our security team?

If Jonathon had been in charge before, would he now work with Michael and Albert?

Those concerns melted away as I opened one of the double doors to Van's master suite. All the items from the trunk and those that had been delivered from the plane were piled just inside the door. The pile didn't hold my attention as much as the room itself.

Setting the wine bottle and glasses on a small round table, I found myself drawn into Van's private sanctuary. Much like the suite I'd been using, the first room was what I'd consider a small living area or study. This one also had a large built-in fireplace, but unlike mine, the woodwork was darker, a rich mahogany custom designed with ornate trim, a stark contrast to the light-colored walls. Two walls were filled with built-in shelving, primarily filled with books.

Even a quick peek let me know that these weren't books simply placed for decoration. The shelves were lined with paperbacks and hardcovers alike in no particular order. Many of the spines were cracked. Pulling one book from a stack of trade paperbacks, I opened the cover, finding the dog-eared pages.

These books weren't embellishments but rather books Van had read.

I ran my fingertips over the spines, reading titles I recognized and more I didn't.

The leather furniture was comfortable and more worn than the furniture in my suite.

Feeling the soft grain, I wondered how much time he spent alone in here before I arrived. Margaret had mentioned that she and her mother worried about him being lonely.

Would a man wealthy enough to own a large estate find comfort within this smaller space?

One wall was covered with slender long blinds.

After a moment of discovery, I found a switch that caused them to pivot and move. Hidden behind the sleek coverings was a wall of glass. It opened in an accordion fashion until all the panes of glass disappeared behind the exterior wall, opening the room to a balcony. I started to open the door when I remembered the security upgrade.

If I moved the latch, would I set off alarms or sirens or whatever extreme measure Van had authorized? Pressing my eyes close to the glass, I made out a hot tub upon the balcony.

My mind quickly went to ideas involving the two of us, a hot bubbling spa, and soft snowflakes. It wasn't until I'd given that some thought that I recalled Van's wish, or more accurately, his order. "Bed. Naked. Waiting."

My thought wasn't verbatim, but the idea was the same.

So far, I hadn't even found the bed.

Grabbing the bottle of wine and glasses, I stepped down the hallway. In my suite, this led to the bathroom and the bedroom. This hallway was longer with other doorways. With my hands full, I continued straight ahead until the hardwood transitioned to plush carpeting.

Twice as large as the bedroom in my suite, this bedroom was spacious with a large bed as the centerpiece, the tall headboard flush against the far wall. In reality, his furnishings were regular bedroom furnishings, yet they all seemed oversized. Or maybe I was a character from the novel *Alice in Wonderland,* and I'd shrunk upon entering Van's private space.

As in the front room, the windows were also covered by sleek blinds operated by a switch. The fireplace in this room was smaller than the one in the front room. After setting the wine and glasses down, I began opening doors.

My first discovery was a large walk-in closet.

A smile came to my lips as I perused his meticulous organization. Unlike his bookshelf, everything was arranged by style and color. I ran my hands over his expensive suits and over his flannel shirts. Even his ties were folded and separated in small compartments within built-in drawers. "You're a very organized man, Van," I mused to myself.

My next discovery was a small workout room with a treadmill and weights. His en-suite bath was in proportion to the rest of his suite, including a spacious glass shower and a sunken tub that could double as a lap pool for someone my size.

With one door left unchecked, I heard the opening of the main door. My pulse clicked faster at the realization I hadn't done as he'd asked. Kicking my boots to the side of the room, I hurried up onto the large bed and pulled my sweater from my frame.

When I turned, Van was standing in the doorway, his one arm on the doorjamb with an almost sinister grin and twinkle to his eyes.

"I...I was looking around." I shrugged. "I told you I'd never been in here."

"Hmm."

The dryness was back, making swallowing difficult. "Did you bring the food?"

Van nodded.

With each passing second the silence grew until the absence of sound roared within my ears accompanied by the swish-swish of my own circulation and the pounding of my heart against my breastbone. Tugging my upper lip with my teeth, I reached for the hem of my silk camisole.

"No."

My hands froze in place. "Van..."

Letting go of the doorjamb, he gestured with his curled finger, bidding me closer.

"I thought you wanted..."

The shake of his head could have been missed, and yet my senses were suddenly on high alert. I hadn't intended to not comply with his demand. I'd meant to do as he'd wished. My intended compliance wasn't only to get my three answers but also because I wanted whatever he had planned.

Now things felt different—heightened.

The deed was done. I'd failed.

And yet as Van's green stare consumed me, my skin tingled, my nipples beaded, and my twisted core dampened.

The air within the room crackled with anticipation as I made my way off the bed. My stocking feet contacted the soft carpet only a millisecond before Van was beside me. With one finger, he lifted my chin until our gazes met.

"Were my directions difficult to follow?"

I shook my head.

"What did I ask?"

"Bed. Naked. Waiting." I hoped those were his words. I veiled my eyes and tilted my face to the side. "Two out of three."

Van's forehead furrowed as he reached for the hem of my camisole. "Contrary to a song you probably don't know, two out of three *is* bad."

I couldn't think of what song he meant, nor did I care. The meaning was clear.

"Bad?" I repeated.

"As in not good." His tone held an element I hoped could be construed as jest. However, that wasn't revealed in his expression.

Willingly, I lifted my arms as he pulled the camisole up and over my head. The cooler air, combined with the heat in his gaze, caused my already tightened nipples to turn diamond hard. Slowly, Van swept my length of hair over each shoulder, fully exposing my breasts.

He didn't need to tell me that he was in control of whatever would happen. He didn't need to direct me to obey. With each breath that became more and more difficult to take, I freely submitted.

Falling to his knees before me, he reached for the button of my gray slacks. My eyes closed as he tugged the button free and lowered the delicate small zipper. Soon the slacks fell, creating a puddle around my ankles. His warm breath teased my skin as his fingers splayed on my hips.

"You're fucking gorgeous, Julia."

I sucked in a breath as he lowered the lace panties he'd given me. My knees wobbled as he leaned toward my core and inhaled. "So sweet."

One by one, he removed my socks until not a stitch of clothing remained.

Standing, he offered me his hand. Placing mine in his large palm, I stepped away from the clothes. Lifting our hands, he encouraged me to turn. Such as a small ballerina in a child's jewelry box, I pirouetted.

Once.

Twice.

Three times.

I was a puppet and Van controlled the strings.

With each turn, my heart rate accelerated, the breath caught in my chest, and my thighs grew damp.

When he stopped my motion, I gasped as he turned me toward the bed. With pressure between my shoulder blades, I bent forward until my breasts flattened against the soft comforter and firm mattress.

"This is what I asked."

I didn't reply.

I couldn't.

Van's touch was everywhere.

Arranging my hair, his hand caressed my neck, my shoulders, and trailed down my spine. Each and every nerve ending was on overdrive as he positioned me exactly to his liking. He cupped each leg, moving from my ankles to the apex. Over and over, he ran his palm over my bottom. One side and the other.

Only my breasts were left unattended as I stayed bent against the mattress.

I was so consumed by his ministrations I didn't anticipate the sting as his palm made contact with my behind. I yelped as the shock and bite of his spank traveled through my consciousness. My feet scrambled as I tried to stand.

Leaning over me, the weight of Van's body kept me in place as his deep tenor reverberated through me. "Remember, we have guests."

Guests.

I couldn't think past this room.

A master puppeteer, Van had me strung so high I felt ready to snap.

Before I could articulate my command for him to stop, I received a second and third swat. The sound of each strike was worse than the sensation. As a matter of fact, the sting lessened, making the flesh of my behind ultra-sensitive as two fingers plunged deep inside me.

"You're soaked," he murmured between kisses to my neck.

The sound of his zipper was almost missed as his voice filled the air. "Are you ready for the orgasms I promised?"

I nodded as I tried to speak.

His hand covered my lips as he buried himself deep inside me, keeping my scream only between us.

Chapter 13

Julia

Waking in Van's large bed, the room around me was as dark as it had been when we'd finally given into sleep. Rolling to my side, I reached for him as I'd done throughout the night. The sheets were empty and cool. I blinked, trying to find a clock. Small numbers on the bedside stand let me know that I'd managed to sleep until after nine.

Stretching my arms and legs upon the soft sheets, I recalled our nighttime activities with the added benefit of time and perspective. Saying that Van continued to take me to new and exhilarating sexual highs seemed as redundant and recurring as declaring the rise of the morning sun.

And still it was true.

A day or even an hour before we arrived home, if I'd been asked how I would react to what Van did to me last night, I would have said it wouldn't happen. My mind told me that spanking was off-limits. We were a couple, equals.

That answer would have been given without the benefit of hindsight.

It wouldn't have considered the shift that our roles make when we're intimate. The concept of our stark alteration in dynamics was difficult to comprehend. In all other aspects of our life together, I felt his equal and his partner. That commonality of mutual respect was one of the aspects missing when Phillip pretended to be Van.

Maybe it was the power of suggestion, but even this morning on the soft sheets, my bottom tingled and my grin grew with the memories of last night.

The answer I would have given would have deprived me of the pleasure Van brought me. The fullness of his cock, combined with the tenderness of his body upon my sensitive skin, was indescribable. He'd awakened every synapse, every nerve. The resulting sensory overload could be felt from the top of my head to the tips of my toes.

By the time we settled to sleep, my body was satisfied in every way possible.

The wine, dip, and bruschetta abated my hunger.

Van's command of my body and the granting of orgasms satiated every other need.

As I lifted the soft covers, I made a mental note to not fret over Van's demands in the future. If last night was any indication, I'd willingly disobey.

Still nude, I walked to the place where I'd found the switch to open the blinds.

As I activated the mechanism, the blinds pivoted and streams of bright sunlight infiltrated the darkness until the blinds moved to the side, no longer obscuring the glass. Bright blue sky contrasted the snow-covered large bowl of Chequamegon Bay beyond the windows. My fingers met the tempered glass as my eyes adjusted to the influx of light.

"If you continue to dress like that, I'll have to cancel my day."

A smile filled my expression as I turned to the handsome man in the doorway. "I didn't hear you enter."

Van placed a tray on a table near the fireplace before walking my way.

From the long strides of his suit-covered legs, to his freshly shaved cheeks and combed dark mane, I took him in. A fresh clean scent, mixed with the light, spicy aroma of cologne, preceded his approach. His shirt was without wrinkle and his satin tie reflected the sunlight. Without the benefit of any covering, I had the sense that I was prey being stalked by a much more dangerous predator. His palm came gently to my cheek seconds before his lips met mine.

Coffee and mint.

"I think I need a shower," I said with a grin when our kiss ended.

"You're beautiful. I wasn't sure if you'd be awake." His grin grew. "We were up a bit late last night. Or I was."

I inclined my cheek toward his touch. "I'm not complaining."

He tilted his head toward the tray. "I wanted to bring you breakfast and coffee. In case you were still asleep, I was trying to be quiet."

Warmth filled my cheeks. "I think I failed in the quiet department last night."

Van's smile grew as he held on to my waist. "I love the noises you make and the words you try to articulate as you're coming apart. Everything about you is genuine."

I let my forehead fall to his chest, landing on his tie. "I'm so happy we're here." I looked up. "What if things had gone differently yesterday?"

"They should have. You never should have been taken." His body tensed. "I promise you, Julia, they'll pay for what they've done."

I shook my head. "Van, if what happened was Phillip's retaliation for something you did in the past, I think we should stop the succession." I laid my hand on his chest, feeling the steady drumbeat of his heart. "I love you. Nothing he did could stop that. I don't want to live in a constant cycle of retaliation. Let's spend our energy on each other."

Van took a deep breath.

"I'm not asking," I went on, "for you to make up and be friends. I'm asking you to concentrate on what we have."

Van ran his finger over my cheek, down my neck,

and between my breasts. "You have a heart of gold. I don't know why you were dropped into my cold, hard world, but I want you to know, I'll never let you go."

Wrapping my arms around his waist, I looked up. A smile lifted my cheeks as I stared up at the way the sun coming through the windows reflected in Van's eyes. "I'm not letting you go either. You can hold onto me for my heart of gold, and I'll hold onto you to see what I'm seeing now."

"And what is that?"

"An explosion of the golden flecks in your gaze. It's magical. I didn't realize how drawn I am to it until I thought it was gone. The flecks say so much. They tell me you love me, desire me, and respect me. They tell me that I'm important without you saying a word."

"It's all true, Julia."

"If red sin is a thing," I said, "maybe this is gold lust."

Van leaned forward, dropping a kiss to the top of my head. "I like that." He took a step back. "Holding your naked body against me isn't exactly going to make my day productive."

My arms fell to my sides. "Here's the thing. I'm now in a suite that doesn't have any of my belongings."

"Then I suppose naked it is."

Scattered over the plush carpet were pieces of our clothing from the night before. Going to the button-up Van had worn yesterday, I lifted it from the floor. "I suppose, I can wear your shirt."

"I'm not sure that will expedite my departure."

"What about our guests?" I asked as I pushed my hands through the armholes.

"They've accepted the position on a temporary trial basis. We'll see what the future brings. Jonathon took them to the guesthouse, and Mrs. Mayhand is already working to make sure they have food."

"Mrs. Mayhand," I murmured, recalling how Phillip called her Paula. "Today is Friday." It wasn't a question, and yet it was. Yesterday was one of those days that seemed to go on for a week.

Van watched as I buttoned the front of his shirt. "It is. Margaret is downstairs, but Mrs. Mayhand will be later."

"Does Margaret know I'm now in your suite?"

"Ours and yes."

"Is our wedding still on for next Saturday in the cabin?"

"It seems as though we have a wedding license purchased in Illinois."

"I'm not getting married in Illinois, Mr. Sherman. I want to be married in Wisconsin." With the front of the shirt buttoned, I began to roll the sleeves before peering up at Van. "Don't get any ideas. If I'm staying in this suite, I'll need my real clothes."

"Oh, beautiful, I have many ideas, all of which would cause me to be even later to the office." He tilted his head toward the front room. "Most of what is out there in those bags is yours from Chicago. There are also the things in the other suite. If you want, I'll ask Margaret to help you get unpacked and move your things."

I shook my head, walking into the large closet I'd seen last night. "I don't need help." I looked down at the cotton shirt and back. "Coffee, breakfast, a shower... that's what I need." Standing in the center, I looked around at all of Van's clothes. "It's just that everything is so organized. I don't want to mess it up."

Leaning against the doorjamb to the closet, Van grinned. "I believe there's room enough to share. Besides, you're my favorite mess."

"Okay, but when you can't find your boxer briefs, don't complain."

He nodded. "I'll go commando."

"Hmm. That idea has possibilities."

Van sucked in a breath. "I have meetings in town and things to catch up on since we've been away. The house is secure and between Jonathon and the others, you have no need to worry about your safety."

"Is...?" I hesitated.

"Go on?"

"Is Phillip still in Chicago? What does everyone know? Could he come here?"

Van wrapped his arm around me. "The PI found where he's staying in Chicago. From what I've learned, he slipped out of your parents' home after we left."

"And Arnold told my parents the truth of what happened?"

Van nodded. "My information has been spotty. We'll get it all worked out."

My shoulders drooped. "The world thinks I walked out on another wedding."

"No one's opinion matters."

"Wade?"

"Your laptop is with the things. Unpack or keep up on your research. You, my dear, are your own boss."

I pursed my lips, holding back a grin. "Not always."

"Let me know if you have any complaints. Remember, we established that the day you moved in. Any complaints by either of us should be brought to the other."

"No complaints."

Van reached for my hand. "Come downstairs and let me show you something before I leave."

"Do you have to leave?" Even I could hear the neediness in my tone.

"I'll be back before too late. When I do, I'll bring you your phone."

I tugged my lower lip. "I'll be alone without a phone?"

"Margaret is here." Tugging on my hand, he winked. "You're covered in my shirt. Come downstairs."

I padded a step behind as Van led me past the bathroom door, the tray of food and coffee, and out to the hallway, landing, and down the stairs until we passed through the French doors. Beside the inside of the front door was another sensor.

Van motioned to the sensor with a keypad. "Jonathon will come by and program your handprint. For now, to unlock or lock the doors enter your birthdate."

"Isn't that an obvious PIN?"

"Do you have a better idea?"

"Twelve eighteen."

"Should I know what that signifies?"

"It's the date of the blizzard. The date we found one another."

Van stepped to the keypad and pushed buttons. "There, your birthday is gone. The code is twelve eighteen." He kissed my hair. "If someone comes to the house and you need help, enter 1-2-3-4. It's the emergency code. The security team will be notified. It's a direct signal to Michael, Albert, and Jonathon. It's faster than the phone."

I nodded. "1-2-3-4. I can remember that."

"Van, I'd like to call Vicki. I want to hear from her what happened yesterday at the house."

"Use the land line or if you want to wait, I'll either bring the new phone as soon as I can or I'll send it with one of the men."

I reached for his hand. "Will you be safe?"

"Don't worry about me, Julia. Only the good die young. I'll live forever."

"You're a good man."

His lips came together as we walked back into the house, closing the glass French doors behind us.

I watched as he donned his suit coat, one lying on a chair, and put it over his shirt. Next was his long gray wool coat. "I don't want to leave you."

"Who's your boss?" Before he could answer, I remembered something. "Wait, I didn't get my three questions last night."

Van's smile quirked. "That was part of your punishment for not doing as I said."

"That's not fair. I took the other punishment."

"Yes, you did. Judging by how wet you were, you didn't hate it. I'm not sure it was a deterrent."

Warmth crawled up my chest, neck, and cheeks as I listened for Margaret. Lowering my tone, I admitted, "I didn't hate it. And I've already been thinking how to provoke it again." I reached for his hand. "Just tell me birth order."

"I was third."

I took a step back. "Third. Is Olivia older than you and Phillip?"

"By minutes. We were born via C-section."

"Wait, what? All three of you? You're a triplet?"

Van nodded. "Obviously, Olivia isn't identical in any way."

"A triplet," I said again, processing the information. "Third?"

"Why is that significant?" he asked.

"I don't know. I guess I thought you'd be first. You know, the overachiever."

"No, Julia, the deck was stacked against me since

before birth. However, I haven't let any of that stand in my way."

I reached for the banister, ready to go back upstairs. "I still have two more questions."

Van came close, giving me a kiss. "Make a list. We can work out a bartering system."

"Bartering?"

His smile grew. "Maybe like strip poker. For each answer, you remove an article of clothing."

"I suppose I should dress in layers." Looking up at his handsome features, I grinned. "I love you no matter what you've done or overcome, Donovan Sherman. Hurry back. I know I'm safe. I just like having you near."

Chapter 14

Van

The moment I stepped into my office, Connie was at the door.

"Mr. Sherman."

Leaving my topcoat on the hall tree, I opened the door, facing my trusted assistant. Connie began working for me when I first set up an office in Ashland. Through the years she'd been an asset in every capacity. As Sherman and Madison grew, so did her responsibilities. However, never had I intended for her job to affect her personal life, not as it had the last week.

"Come in, Connie." I stopped, looking at the only other person who knew more about me than I usually shared. Her brown eyes met mine. "How are you?" I asked.

With a deep breath, she stood tall. "I'm good. Thank you. I wanted to thank you for helping with Phillip and so does Eric."

I motioned to the chairs across from my desk. "Have a seat." I looked at the coffee machine on the credenza. "Would you like a cup of coffee?"

"I think that's my job," she said, taking a seat. "Is Ms. McGrath okay?"

I nodded. "She is. You were right."

"I was?"

"She knew he wasn't me. I should have told her about Phillip, but she still knew something was wrong."

Connie's smile grew. "A woman knows the man she loves."

I popped a K-cup in the coffee maker and hit the start button. Taking the chair beside Connie, I offered her my apologies. "You shouldn't have had to deal with Phillip. I'm sorry he contacted your private phone."

"The man who traced the calls told me to block him." Connie looked down at her hands in her lap and back up. "I was afraid if I blocked him, he'd retaliate. Do you think that's why he went after Ms. McGrath? If it's my fault—"

"No," I interrupted. "Nothing regarding Phillip Thomas is your fault. Don't worry about that. The blame is his and his alone. Can you tell me why you thought he may be dangerous?"

Her lips came together in a straight line for a moment before she spoke. "He demanded to talk to you. He said you owed him and that you'd pay. When he called my personal phone, he mentioned my daughter and two grandchildren among other things."

I gripped the arm of the chair. "Connie, it's your choice, but I'd like you to file a police report."

"You would?"

I nodded.

"Mr. Sherman, I told Eric that you wouldn't want the publicity. I told him we'd let you handle it, and Phillip would go away."

I'd like to make him go away.

"I'd like to pretend I could do that," I said. Letting out a breath, I sat back and unbuttoned my suit coat as I recalled Julia's request to end the cycle of revenge. "As you know, I've handled things with my family more directly in the past." There was no way to hide everything from Connie. "Things are different now."

"Speaking of why, I hope Ms. McGrath liked the dress for the New Year's Eve party."

"You are a lifesaver as usual. She did like it and she was stunning. I'll support you with your decision regarding the police. Did you save any of his voicemails?"

"Eric thought it was a good idea."

"I agree. Turn them over to the police."

Connie sat forward. "I think you should listen to them first."

"Me?"

She nodded. "In one that lasted over four minutes, he divulged more than you may want public."

Fuck.

"Who has heard it?" I asked.

Her head shook from side to side. "I let Eric listen. I was so distraught, I wasn't—"

"Connie, I trust you, and I trust Eric. I'm starting to

understand that when two people care about one another, they don't keep secrets. I wouldn't ask you to deceive your husband."

"Mr. Sherman, there's a line between personal and business. Eric doesn't ask about particulars of Sherman and Madison, and I don't offer them. Just as I don't ask about particulars of his work. We've found a happy medium. I'm sure you and Ms. McGrath will find that too. This was different. Phillip said things about you and about my family. He knew things about my grand-children. I suppose he could have found them on social media." She shook her head. "I don't like all that the kids share nowadays." Her brown gaze met mine. "I had to wonder if since what he said about my family was accurate, if his accusations about you were too."

"I don't know until I listen."

She stood. "I'll let you listen and then decide if you still want to include the police."

I also stood. "I can't thank you enough for your loyalty."

A smile took over her concerned expression. "I think you sent me a text about a raise. You said for me to remind you."

"You're right, I did."

Connie looked down at her watch. "Your first appointment, a Mr. Michael Ricks, is due any minute."

"He's going to be helping me personally as well as working with Sherman and Madison's security team to make sure we're doing all we can to avoid situations like yesterday or Phillip's calls. I wanted to include Flora Banks in our meeting."

"I can patch her through." As she started to leave, Connie stopped and turned my way. "Ms. McGrath's phone is here. Unfortunately, I couldn't get her previous number transferred."

"Why?"

"Her other phone is still active."

"It shouldn't be. Have it deactivated."

"It's not under her name. The account is in her parents' names. Without the account holder's consent..."

I inhaled. "I'm going to make a call. I'll let you know when to send Michael back and contact Ms. Banks."

"Mr. Sherman."

"Yes."

She broadened her smile. "I'm very happy for you and Ms. McGrath."

"Thank you. Me too."

"I can tell."

I stood for a moment as the door closed, torn between wondering what Phillip's voicemail revealed and how it would work to help me achieve my new plan.

My brother was insane.

There was no other reason he would pretend to be me.

Delusional.

His attempt to defraud Julia and her parents was witnessed by others.

If Madison was no longer fit to raise Brooklyn, and Phillip was delusional or deemed dangerous, then the custody of Brooklyn would need to be reevaluated. Living with Liv would be better for her.

Granted, this plan was in its early stages, but it was a plan. Instead of taking on the revenge myself, maybe I could let the legal and social systems work their magic. I'd just give them a little push in the right direction.

Calling from my office landline, I dialed Gregg McGrath. I'd yet to hear directly all that transpired yesterday. There was also the minor issue of canceling and deactivating Julia's phone from the McGraths' account.

As I waited for the call to connect, I logged into my computer and scanned the magnitude of unread emails. I'd cleared them all in the car before we arrived home. One caught my eye. It was from an Ashley at Green-Sphere dot com.

Before I could open the email, Gregg answered. "Gregg McGrath."

"Donovan."

He sighed. "Yes, I've been waiting for your call."

I supposed he was waiting to hear my side. "Yesterday was a shitshow. My twin would never have made his way into your house with Julia without outside help. You know that, right?"

Gregg's voice lowered. "I don't know what to believe anymore. Tell me that Julia is safe."

"She is."

"If this call is about the balloon payment, I'm prepared to put another lien on our home if you require immediate repayment."

I stood and paced near the windows. "I don't want repayment."

"Julia told us that you were demanding it since she..."

"Julia *told you*," I repeated. "When?"

"Yesterday, after you left with her. She texted and explained about your brother—Phillip is his name, right?"

Fuck.

"Gregg, listen to me carefully. Julia has been with me since we left your house. She doesn't have her phone."

"Has she told you that she's changed her mind about marriage, to you or to Skylar?"

"No, she hasn't. If a text message said that, it wasn't from her. She had no way to contact you via text. Phillip took her phone."

"That doesn't make sense," Gregg said. "I have the text messages, including the alarming one this morning."

Alarming?

"Phillip must have sent them."

"What about the raid on your plane?"

My head shook. "It wasn't a raid. It was a delay tactic. Wires were crossed. My security alerted the police that Phillip may try to take Julia to the plane after forcing the wedding. My assistant didn't get that message. Everything has been worked out. You need to have Julia's phone deactivated immediately. If Phillip is sending messages to you and Ana, he could be contacting others as well, pretending he's Julia."

Gregg's voice lowered to a whisper. "What the fuck, Sherman? After what she sent this morning, we're beside ourselves. I need to speak to my daughter."

"You will. I promise. I also promise she's safe."

"I want confirmation."

"Fuck, Gregg, Julia isn't in danger now. She was when she was in your house, and you did nothing to stop it."

"Donovan, you should know, our attorney advised against involving law enforcement. He said to wait for your demands, but after today's text, we couldn't."

"What the fuck are you saying? Law enforcement? My demands? My only demand is to disconnect her cell number."

"Julia said she..." He cleared his throat. "Donovan, I don't care who you are or what you can do to Wade. Julia is our daughter. I swear to God, I'll fight you."

My grip of the handset tightened. "What did her text say?"

"She confessed she is frightened. She's worried you won't let her leave. She said you hurt her." His tone deepened. "Face the fact, she doesn't want to marry you."

"Gregg, Julia isn't harmed. Our wedding isn't cancelled." I hurried to my overcoat. "I'm headed back to her right now. You'll be able to speak to her in less than fifteen minutes."

"I need proof," Gregg said, "I've contacted the Wisconsin State Patrol. Taking her over a state line without her consent—"

Disconnecting the call, I tossed the receiver onto my desk. Donning my coat, I stepped toward Connie's office and my gaze met Michael's. "Come with me. We're headed to the house."

"Mr. Sherman, your schedule," Connie said.

"Give me Julia's new phone."

Connie retrieved a bag from beneath her desk and handed it my way. "Your schedule?"

"Tell Ms. Banks that Michael will be in touch. For now, reschedule anything else today for virtual. I'm not leaving Julia." Not if the Wisconsin State Patrol are on their way. I didn't add that information. "Also, Connie, check with Sherman and Madison PR. Phillip has Julia's phone and may be pretending to be her in an online presence. Have them scouring the social media platforms." I looked at Michael who was now standing. "Come with me. I'll explain on the way."

Chapter 15

Julia

Wrapping a towel around me, I wiped the steam from the large mirror over the vanity. Obviously, I didn't think everything out. My items in this suite were still packed.

With my hair wet and dripping down my shoulders, I walked out to the pile of luggage in the front room. The simplest solution was to go to my old suite.

Securing the towel, I stepped into the hallway beyond the master bedroom suite. Sunshine filled the landing as I paused and listened for Margaret down below. She knew I'd moved suites. That didn't mean I wanted to run into her or our new security staff dressed in only a towel.

The house was quiet as I made my way to my old suite.

Opening the door, I smiled at the front room, thinking how I'd finally allow Margaret to clean it once I had my things down to the other suite. My first order of business was getting dressed. Walking into a closet a fourth of the size of Van's, I remembered his bartering comment.

Layers.

Once I had panties, soft leggings, warm socks, a camisole, and sweater on, I went into the bathroom to do something with my long, wet, and tangled mess of hair.

My thoughts were consumed with the present and future.

Van wasn't only a twin. He was a triplet.

What happened to cause the break with his siblings and family?

Madison married Phillip.

Did that mean that Brooklyn was Madison and Phillip's daughter?

The questions came faster than the answers.

It would be too easy to get bogged down in what happened yesterday. I could go down the rabbit hole of Van and Phillip's feud. There were things Van had done, things he now regretted. The picture that had been in his office came to mind. I wondered where it had gone. Now that I knew it was Phillip and Madison, I wanted to see it again.

Leaning forward, I peered at my reflection. "Stop."

The answers would come, but that wasn't what was important. What mattered was that Van and I were home. Our wedding was going to happen on our terms. The most important thing I learned yesterday was that without a doubt I loved Donovan Sherman.

The Donovan Sherman.

It wasn't his good looks, his money, or anything else. Phillip pretended to embody all that Van allowed others to see. He fooled Albert and my parents because they don't know the real Van. He didn't fool me.

My love is for the man, his caring nature, his protectiveness, and the lust I feel when I stare into his gold-speckled green gaze.

After a smidge of mascara, blush, and lip color, I began to tackle my hair. Georgette was probably right. I should send for some of the products she recommended. The hair dryer echoed off the tile as I began to dry my hair, combing and brushing as I worked.

The funny thing about a hair dryer was that it was easy to forget how truly loud it was. The din it created settled in my thoughts, drowning out everything else until I turned it off.

Voices.

Loud voices.

My pulse sped up at the echo of footsteps pounding down the hallway.

Margaret?

The footsteps were too heavy to be hers.

"Oh, please, don't let Margaret be hurt."

The door to my old suite banged against the wall from a room away. My hands trembled as my gaze darted around the bathroom. There was nowhere for me to hide.

Can I make it to the bedroom?

No. The footsteps were coming closer.

Shit.

My gaze went to the doorknob. The door wasn't locked.

I took a step closer and immediately back.

It was too late.

Another step back. My shoulders collided with the wall as I lifted my only means of defense—the blow dryer.

What am I going to do, blow this person away on the top speed?

I held my breath as the bathroom door flung open.

"Fuck, Julia. Why didn't you answer? Why are you down here?"

I tried to make sense of Van's reappearance.

"Why are you back already?" I looked at the vanity. "My stuff is in here. I was going to move it after I dressed."

Van's arms came around me, pressing my weapon of choice to my stomach and holding me tight. When he loosened his grip, I grinned down at the hair dryer. "You're lucky I didn't get you with this."

He took the dryer from my grasp, placing it on the vanity. "Fuck. You need to call your dad."

"Okay," I said tentatively. "Is it an emergency?"

"Yes." He handed me a phone.

Opening the screen, I saw that my numbers were gone. "Where's all my information?"

"On your other phone."

My gaze narrowed. "The one Phillip took?"

"Here." He swiped his phone, brought up my dad's number and handed it to me.

My hands resumed their trembling as I grasped the phone. "What's the emergency?" The breakfast and coffee from earlier churned in my stomach. "Is Dad all right? Is it Mom?"

"No, it's you. Call him."

I hit the call icon.

Me?

"Donovan," my father's voice answered.

"No, Dad. It's me. Are you all right?"

"Little girl. Are you safe? Has he hurt you? Your mother and I want you home. Don't worry. The police are on their way. We can move forward..."

I hit the speaker icon. "Dad, what police? I'm fine. I'm good. Arnold was supposed to tell you that I was safe with Van."

"He did. It was your text messages. Don't worry about the balloon payment. All that matters is you."

"Balloon payment?" I looked up at Van in question. "Dad, I haven't texted you."

Mom's voice came onto the call. "Julia."

I took a deep breath. The last time I'd spoken to her, she was telling me to marry Skylar. "Mom, I'm safe."

"Why are you calling on Donovan's phone?" Her volume lowered. "Is he forcing you to say you're safe? Did he threaten you? Has he hurt you?"

Van's phone began dinging with incoming messages.

I turned back to him, my eyes open wide, searching for answers. "What is happening?"

Mom continued, "Julia, we told the police everything. They're on their way. They can help you."

"Help me what, Mom? I'm literally standing in a bathroom, drying my hair, and about to unpack. Unless you called the police to help me unpack, I don't understand."

"Is he listening? If you can't talk freely, say dress."

My mother was giving me a safe word.

"Julia, come home."

"I'm home, Mom." I hit the disconnect button. "What the hell?" I asked Van.

He took the phone from me and began reading the onslaught of text messages. "Fuck, Julia. Come downstairs."

"What is happening?" I asked again.

"Text messages were sent to your parents by you—your phone—claiming you were afraid of me. I hurt you. I think because you supposedly broke off the engagement. Your dad thought I'd demanded the balloon payment be reimbursed."

"Phillip."

Van nodded.

"Who's downstairs?" I asked.

"According to Albert, there are two uniformed state patrol officers at the gate. I just texted for him to allow them entry. I'd say they'll be at our door in a minute or two."

As we stepped from the bathroom, I saw Michael down the hallway near the landing.

I reached for Van's hand. "Was he looking for me too? I heard voices."

"I think we panicked Margaret as well."

We headed toward the staircase. "Why would Phillip do this?" I asked.

"Because he thinks he has nothing left to lose. The thing is that he's wrong. But when I'm done, he'll be right. He'll have nothing left."

"Van, I don't want this to go on."

Van stood taller, his chest inflating with his deep breath. "It won't. I promise."

The ring of the doorbell echoed from down below.

"The police are here," he said, squeezing my hand. "I'm sure they'll want to speak to you alone."

"I'm sorry my parents—"

Van shook his head. "All they have to do is trace the phone to know the texts weren't sent from here."

Once we reached the bottom of the step, Michael asked, "Do you want me to answer the door?"

"No," Van replied. "I will."

Chapter 16

Julia

"*P*atrol Officers," Van said in way of greeting.

Standing at the open French doors, I felt as if I were watching a movie or television show. The officers' expressions were serious as the male officer spoke to Van. His voice was too low for me to hear.

If this visit was about me, I should be at the door too.

"Hello," I greeted as I came up behind Van.

"Ms. McGrath?" the female patrol officer asked.

"Yes, I'm Julia McGrath."

"Ma'am, we'd like to talk to you—outside."

The cold air from beyond the door was already entering the house. Wrapping my arms around myself, I looked down at my stocking-covered feet. "I'm sorry, I'm not dressed." I looked up at Van and then added, "Come inside."

"Are you inviting us in?" the male patrolman asked.

"Come in," Van said, gesturing to the living room.

After stamping the snow from their boots in the foyer, the two patrol officers joined Van and I inside. We weren't alone. Michael and Margaret were watching from the kitchen doorway.

"I'm Patrolman Stewart," the man said. "And this is Patrol Officer Howard." Van and I nodded.

"I appreciate your visit," I began. "I spoke briefly to my parents. There's been a misunderstanding."

"Mr. Sherman," Patrolman Stewart said, "may I have a few words with you?"

"And Ms. McGrath," Patrol Officer Howard said, "if we could speak alone?"

"We can speak in my office," Van offered Patrolman Stewart. He gave my hand a squeeze before leading Officer Stewart down the hallway.

Officer Howard waited until they disappeared around a corner. Her gaze went toward the kitchen where Michael and Margaret had been standing. "Is this private enough for you to speak freely?"

I shook my head as I went to one of the sofas near the windows and gestured for her to join me. "Officer Howard, I don't need privacy. This is all a misunderstanding."

She removed an electronic tablet from a pouch attached to her belt. "Your parents forwarded the text messages that you sent."

"I didn't send any text messages. I lost my phone yesterday." I pulled the new one from a pocket in my leggings. "See, I have a new one."

"May I see that?"

I handed it to her.

"This phone is wiped clean. Did you do that, or did someone persuade you to eliminate your contacts against your will?"

"It's not wiped clean. It's brand new. Yesterday, I gave my phone to someone I mistakenly trusted. I never got it back. Any text messages sent by my old number were sent by him."

"Who is this person?" she asked.

I couldn't come up with a reason to be anything less than truthful. "My fiancé's brother."

"You gave him your phone?"

"It's a bit complicated," I said with a scoff. "You see, I didn't know until yesterday that my fiancé has a twin."

"How would you not know that?"

"That answer too is complicated. The point is that my fiancé's twin brother led me to believe he was my fiancé. He asked for my phone, and I gave it to him."

"Did you ask for it back?"

"No, I left my parents' home before I had the opportunity."

Patrol Officer Howard looked around the large living room. "Did you leave your parents' home of your own free will?"

"Yes."

"Did Mr. Sherman force you to leave?"

"Isn't that the same question?"

"Ms. McGrath, we want to understand what prompted the text messages."

"I don't know what prompted the text messages," I replied. "I didn't send them." As the patrol officer entered information on her tablet, I went on, "Van, Mr. Sherman, and I both wanted to leave my parents' home. It was mutual. You can speak to Mr. and Mrs. Thalmer. They work for my parents and have since I was young. We spoke with Rosemary before we left. She can tell you my state of mind."

"If I spoke to her, what would she say?"

I sighed. "She'd say I left the house willingly. She'd tell you that Mr. Sherman is a good man who promised her he'd..."

"He'd what?"

A smile came to my lips. "He promised to love me, care for me, and encourage me to fly."

"Sometimes," she said, "people say one thing and do another. Has Mr. Sherman hurt you?"

"No."

"Has he struck you?"

The last thing I was going to do was to get into a conversation about bedroom antics. Besides, I didn't think she meant a foreplay spanking. "No, Mr. Sherman has never frightened or harmed me." I lifted my left hand, showing her my ring. "Our engagement is still on. This entire situation is a farce perpetrated by Phillip Thomas, Mr. Sherman's brother. He had my phone and probably still does. Check with the cell provider regarding the text messages. They would have come from Chicago, not Ashland."

Officer Howard stood and handed me a business card. "Here's the number of an agency in Ashland. Anyone you speak to there can help you. Don't be afraid of Mr. Sherman's influence. You are our concern."

Standing, I looked at the card and back to Officer Howard. "I know you're doing your job. I think you're very good at it. I promise you, I'm safe. I'm here because I want to be here. I never sent text messages to my parents claiming otherwise."

"I advise you to have the phone disabled."

I nodded. "As soon as I can."

She offered me her hand. "I apologize for bothering you."

As she spoke, we both turned to the hallway, hearing Van's and Officer Stewart's voices. From their expressions, I gathered his talk went as well as mine, or at least as well as I thought it had.

"Ms. McGrath," Officer Stewart said, "I also apologize for this inconvenience."

I walked to Van's side. "I assure you, I'm where I want to be. There is no place I'd rather be."

He nodded. "We will let you know if we hear of any other concerns."

Officer Howard turned my way with a whispered tone. "Who else did I see when we first entered?"

"They work for us," Van answered. "Margaret Curry is local. Michael Ricks is new."

Both officers nodded. "We'll be on our way," Patrol Officer Howard said. "Have a good day."

Once they'd gone and we'd watched them get into their car, I turned and wrapped my arms around Van's torso. His arms encircled me as I laid my head against his chest. When I looked up, he was staring my direction.

"That was crazy," I said.

Van reached for my hand and teased back the sleeve of my sweater. "He asked me if I'd hurt you."

"You haven't."

"I thought about our Christmas dinner."

I pushed the sleeves up to my elbows. "See, I'm good." A smile lifted my cheeks. "Satin, remember."

"Last night..."

"Van, they wanted to know if you abused me. You haven't and you won't. If enjoying sex beyond missionary were a crime, the jails would be filled."

His smile bloomed as he lifted my chin. "I'm not sure of the statistics, but I like the way you think."

"I don't think. I know. I love you. I woke up wondering how I could possibly have enjoyed what we did as much as I had. My second thought was wondering what I could do to provoke it again."

He kissed my forehead. "What Phillip did yesterday went too far, Julia. I heard what you said about a cycle of retaliation, but I can't let this go. Phillip needs to be stopped."

Pressing my lips together, I nodded. "I agree. I'll call my dad back. I know, I'll send him one of our private emails. Hopefully, he'll finally believe it's me."

"Connie tried to have your old number switched to the new phone. Your name isn't on the account."

"I'll talk to him about that too. Aren't you supposed to be at the office?" I asked.

"I am, but I'm not leaving you."

"I'm fine. Michael and Margaret are here."

Van's forehead furrowed and his nostrils flared.

"What is it?" I asked.

"Officer Stewart put a trace on your phone."

"My old one?"

Van nodded.

"Your private investigator said he knew the hotel in Chicago where Phillip was staying."

"Your phone is pinging in Ironwood."

My heart sped up as my mind scrambled with geography. "I don't know all the towns around here."

"Ironwood, Michigan. It's about forty miles east."

"Michigan?"

Van nodded. "Wisconsin State Patrol doesn't have jurisdiction. They're contacting the Michigan State Police. If this goes further, it will be a federal issue."

My stomach twisted. "Van, this is ridiculous."

"Ironwood is less than an hour away."

I stood straighter. "Are you saying that Phillip could be that close?"

"I don't know. He could be using a VPN to make it appear he's there or fuck, he could be there. I'm calling Rob, the private investigator. I want visual confirmation."

"Please make this stop. Make him stop."

Chapter 17

Van

"I'm telling you what the state patrol officer just told me," I said to Rob Landon, the private detective. "Julia's number is pinging in Ironwood, Michigan."

"It wasn't Phillip. I've been tailing him since this morning."

Letting out a long breath, I sat back against my desk chair. "You're sure? You have visual confirmation?" Yes, I wanted evidence. I wanted more than that. I wanted my brother's head on a fucking platter. That sounded a little Old Testament. Nevertheless, it seemed appropriate—brother against brother.

"Unless you're staying at the DoubleTree," Rob said, "it's him."

My jaw ached from all the clenching. "And you haven't lost sight of him?"

"He went back to his room after lunch. I can tell you what he ordered."

"I don't give a fuck about his diet. I want to know

he didn't jump onto a plane and head to the upper peninsula."

"I just sent you a picture, Mr. Sherman. He took the elevator less than an hour ago. He didn't send text messages from the UP. The man he met with before, Logan Butler, met him in the hotel's restaurant for what appeared to be a working lunch."

My phone vibrated.

Changing the call to speaker, I looked at the picture. There was no doubt I was seeing Phillip and Logan. This picture was clearer than the one he'd sent yesterday.

"Phillip pays for everything in cash," Rob said. "There's only a very small digital imprint that he's in Chicago at all. Nothing more than his airline ticket. And that only means he flew into O'Hare, the same as forty thousand other people in the last forty-eight hours."

"Shit, I'm sure the Wisconsin patrol are going to follow up on what we told them."

"Maybe they can find something I can't."

I tried to recall. "What did you say was the name on the reservations?"

"I didn't. Remember I told you that the money in his account came via layers of shell companies? One of those companies was listed on the reservation."

"What name?"

"MMT Inc."

It rang a bell. "You mentioned that yesterday. It doesn't mean a thing to me."

"All I know is that it was the company that made the deposit in Phillip's account, the same company name on the hotel reservations, and today one of my associates linked it to a SPAC."

My free hand gripped the arm of my chair. "Do you have the name of the SPAC?"

"Yeah, yeah. It's in my notes..."

As I waited, I logged into my office email, remembering the email I'd meant to check before all hell broke loose.

"Here it is," Rob said, "GreenSphere Opportunities."

That information was more than my people had been able to find. "You're saying that MMT Inc. is an investor in GreenSphere Opportunities."

"Does that mean something?"

My head was nodding. "It could." My thoughts were going a million different directions until I remembered Julia's plea. 'Make him stop.'

"How long do you want him tailed?" Rob asked.

Until he takes his last breath. I reconsidered. "Don't stop. Get others on the job if you need to. If and when I call, I want to know exactly where my dear brother is located down to the longitude and latitude."

"Considering the two Long Island Teas he had for lunch, I'm guessing things aren't going as planned."

"He drank his lunch?"

Rob scoffed. "You said you weren't interested in his diet."

What had Phillip said on the phone?

He said he pictured me with my money, drinking myself to death.

Project much, brother? I didn't say that aloud, but the mere thought brought a smile to my face. "Thank you for keeping track of him. Keep his phone monitored too. Make sure it is coming from wherever he's located."

"Will do." Rob paused. "Is your fiancée all right? I should have gotten you that information sooner."

"She's doing well. We all fucked this up. Let's not let it happen again."

"Yes, sir."

I disconnected the call thinking about what I'd just said. I was right. There was plenty of blame to be shared. It also wouldn't do me any good to fire everyone and start from scratch. Hell, I'd fucked up too by not telling Michael that I had a brother who could look like me.

I rocked back against my chair, letting the relief give me a slight reprieve. I spoke aloud, reconfirming what I'd learned. "He's in Chicago."

Does that mean someone else is in Ironwood, or is the answer as simple as a virtual private network?

What is Logan's role in all of this?

Why would the Butlers tank the perceived value of Wade?

The relief didn't last long.

Sending a quick text to my new personal security team, I confirmed Phillip's whereabouts and asked Michael to inform Ms. Banks with Sherman and Madison. My next call was to the loan officer who had taken my balloon payment.

After a redundant five-minute discussion, I convinced him that the news that Julia McGrath was an infamous runaway bride was false. Our wedding was still planned. I was not looking to sell off my shares of Wade Pharmaceutical.

I clicked on the email I'd seen at the office as I wondered who Ashley from GreenSphere was and why she was contacting me. The email was short and to the point. She had an exclusive time-sensitive investment opportunity. She left me a phone number.

Before I called Ashley, I returned another call I meant to return earlier.

Lena answered on the third ring. "Do you have your runaway bride back?"

"Are you joking? I'm not in the mood."

"Does that mean she's still missing?"

Taking my cell phone to the windows, I paced as I talked. "Julia is with me. She's safe. It also means I want Phillip gone for good."

"If you're discussing a murder-for-hire, I don't know a thing. But discreetly, I might have a guy."

"Shit, Lena, you do have all the contacts."

"You never know."

Phillip was Lena's brother-in-law and yet there was no love lost between the two.

"I received an interesting email," I offered. "It came early this morning. I've been a little busy with the Wisconsin State Patrol."

"Shit, what did you do?"

"Nothing...this time. Back to the email. Did you by chance get one?"

"You're going to have to be more specific, Van."

"GreenSphere."

"Oh," Lena said. "I told you, they've been courting me since I acquired my percent of Wade shares. And yes, they contacted me again this morning. I'd assume hoping to buy low."

"I just spoke with the bank. The news of Wade's devaluation is all talk. Wade's credit rating hasn't and won't be affected." I took a breath, looking out at the snow-covered bay. "Logan is coaching Phillip."

"I told you that Logan mentioned him."

"You called Julia the runaway bride. I'm assuming you read the latest?"

"I did. I also knew what you told me yesterday. I figured..."

"He pretended to be me," I explained, getting right to the point. "We believe the plan was to get Julia to marry at her parents' home, Phillip would bail at the last minute, and Skylar Butler would swoop in and save her from a second failed wedding."

Lena's laugh was halfhearted.

"I fail to see the humor."

"It's because you're not looking. Come on. It could have worked."

"To accomplish what? Getting me out of Julia's life?"

"Out of Julia's life," Lena said, "equates to out of Wade. With you gone it removes the spotlight. Logan probably figured you'd walk away and sell your shares in the process."

"Fuck no, I'd bury them all."

"He may have underestimated you."

"We're even," I admitted. "I underestimated them too. The busted attempt at the wedding wasn't enough. Phillip took Julia's phone from her. He contacted her parents as her and claimed she wanted to leave me and I wouldn't let her. The texts said she was scared. I was threatening to keep her against her will...hell, you know the story."

"You do have a history."

Clenching my jaw, I ran my hand over my hair. "That information was never made public."

"Phillip knows. That might mean Logan does too."

I took a deep breath. "Julia isn't being held prisoner."

"Is that why the *Paw Patrol* visited?"

"You lost me on that."

"It's a kids' show. Ask Julia."

I told myself to breathe. "Sometimes you can be a real bitch."

"But you love me."

"If you're asking if the text messages are why the Wisconsin Patrol visited, yes." I went back to the subject of the email. "Have you spoken to the woman from GreenSphere?"

"Not today."

"Have you or Jeremy heard of MMT Inc? It's a shell company."

"Doesn't ring any bells. I can ask him to dig."

"See what you can find out. I'm going to have my guys working on it too. There might be a connection to GreenSphere."

"And what's the connection to Wade?" she asked.

"That's what I want to find out."

Telling Lena that I'd been thinking about what she'd told me about Madison—her declined mental and emotional state—was on the tip of my tongue. That had been lingering in the back of my mind since our conversation. To say my thoughts were consumed with Madison's well-being would be inaccurate. I'd been considering how her mental decline would play in Brooklyn's custody if Phillip were to also be declared unfit. I'd also been thinking that if anyone was pointing fingers to the villain in Madison's decline, no one was immune.

Lena, Logan, Phillip, me, and Madison herself.

"I need to get to the bottom of this," I said. "Phillip has already taken it too far. I'm not letting Julia get fucked like..."

The silence of my unfinished sentence hung in the air.

"Like Madison, Van. Is that what you were going to say?"

"Yes."

"Hmm," Lena recounted. "Literally and figuratively." Her voice took on a more determined tone. "I'm going to go see her."

"I thought you weren't allowed."

"I'm not asking."

"Lord help whoever tries to stop you," I said, knowing that when Lena had a will, she'd find a way.

"It's been too long. I'm a shitty sister. I tried, though, back when—"

"You did, Lena. You aren't a shitty sister any more than I'm a shitty brother."

Her laugh was louder than before. "If that's supposed to be a pep talk, try again."

"No, it's the truth. We can only put up with so much shit before washing our hands. It's the only way to stay sane."

"So you think we're sane?"

I grinned. "I mean, on a scale from one to ten, I'd give us a seven."

"I'll talk to Jeremy about MMT and get back to you."

Hearing the letters from Lena gave them a new perspective. "Fuck," I muttered.

Lena replied, "Oh shit. Are you thinking what I'm thinking?"

"Why? It has to be a coincidence."

"Right," Lena replied. "It's a coincidence that a shell company has Madison's initials."

Madison Montgomery Thomas.

Chapter 18

Julia

Surveying the dwindling number of suitcases and boxes, I tried to concentrate on the task at hand instead of my recent conversation with my parents.

Hopefully, they were finally coming around. Admittedly, the entire episode with Phillip was unnerving and like something out of an old soap opera, the kind my grandmother never missed—disenfranchised twin resurfaces to wreak havoc on the family who did him wrong.

If I could take my parents' word, they both believed Phillip was Van. It wasn't until after Van and I left the house and Arnold told my father what was happening that my dad was even suspicious. I couldn't blame them. I was fooled too, at least on the surface.

Instead of facing my parents or the guests, Phillip slipped out shortly after us. When I asked Dad who else heard Arnold's news, Dad said it was Marlin, confirming Van's suspicions to me. The Butlers knew it was Phillip and tipped him off.

That was the news neither of my parents wanted to

believe. As the evidence mounted against Marlin, my mom's heels dug in, refusing to discuss that he and possibly Uncle Logan deserved any fault.

She had one point I couldn't ignore. She asked why Marlin, as a major stockholder, would want to hurt Wade's worth. The way my mother saw it, I missed the opportunity to right the wrongs of the last month. In one afternoon, I could have gotten Van out of Wade and married the man I'd vowed to love.

The thing was that I never vowed to love Skylar. I stopped it before it went that far.

I shook my head, thinking how she'd rather I were with Skylar than Van.

"More shoes," Margaret said, pulling me from my thoughts.

The pile of suitcases and boxes we'd been unpacking was slowly getting smaller. It wasn't everything I'd packed at my parents. There was more to be delivered, along with my car, but our current effort was a start.

"You don't need to help me unpack," I told Margaret for not the first time. When she turned, I smiled. "But I'm glad you are."

"I don't mind. You two were gone, and the house barely needed cleaning."

I opened a heavy box as Margaret carried the box of shoes back to the master suite closet. Looking at the books and papers within, I sighed. "I think these should stay boxed up."

When Margaret didn't answer, I carried another garment bag to the closet. Pushing past the tall doors, I found Margaret sitting on the floor within, pulling shoe boxes out and stacking them by style. I shook my head as I looked around. "I feel bad taking up so much space."

"Donovan wants you in here. I don't think he'll mind if he loses some closet space. His suits can touch one another. It isn't a sin."

Tugging my lip, I watched as the number of shoe boxes multiplied. It was as if Margaret was pulling them from Mary Poppins's magic bag. "Where can we put them?"

Looking around, she laughed. "Okay, hear me out. This entire section"—she gestured— "with his casual clothes. Imagine that there's a shoe rack or shelves and drawers for the unmentionables you brought from the other suite."

I laughed. "I think we can mention them. You bought them."

"I delivered them," she said. "Donovan picked them out."

Margaret stood and brushed her hands on her blue jeans. "Oh, and I saw this thing in one of Jonathon's magazines. Instead of one clothes rack, it's three. They rotate. I know it sounds odd, but it would work for slacks."

I took a deep breath. "Sometimes, I wish things were easier."

"I didn't want to ask, but the curiosity is killing me. Why were the state patrol officers here?"

Shaking my head as I condensed Van's suits from two racks to one, I debated mentioning Phillip. If I didn't, I would be putting Margaret in the same situation that I'd been in if he came around. Sighing, I replied, "It's a mess."

"It sounded like it ended all right."

"It did because it was a false alarm in the first place. Do you know anything about Van's brother?"

Margaret's lips came together as she contemplated my question. "I know a little."

"I'm not digging. I think you should know." I remembered that Margaret's husband helped with the security. "Van is a twin, a triplet. But his brother is identical."

Margaret nodded.

"You knew?"

"When we first met Donovan, there was family drama." She shrugged. "I haven't met his siblings."

"I met Phillip."

"You did?"

"That was the mess. He pretended to be Van." I thought back to getting in the car, thankful the encounter didn't end worse than it had. "Anyway, while I thought he was Van, I gave him my phone. As far as I know, Phillip still has it. He sent my parents text messages. Since they came from my number, they assumed it was me."

Margaret's expression dimmed. "The texts weren't good, were they?"

I shook my head. "They said I was leaving Van and I was afraid of him. Something about him holding me against my will."

Margaret picked up the empty box. "It's none of my business, but I think you two should get married and shut up all the people telling lies."

"We're going to."

"You are?"

"I mean the wedding isn't planned except in my head. I want to marry in the cabin."

Her eyes opened wide. "As in the cabin without electricity?"

A giggle preceded my answer. "That would be the one."

"Let me guess, it's a daytime wedding."

"Probably. There is the fireplace for light." I shrugged. "I told you it isn't planned."

"When do you want to do this?"

"Next Saturday."

"A week from tomorrow?" she asked, her voice rising an octave.

I grinned at the absurdity of hearing my plan aloud. "I want the wedding small. We were hoping that you, Jonathon, and Paula could come. Oh, and your son."

"You want us there?"

"Yes. I don't know Jonathon, but Van thinks a lot of

him, and you and your mother have been nothing but kind to me."

"Will there be out-of-town guests? I can get the rooms ready. As you know, the doors mostly stay locked."

I shook my head. "I don't think there will be any guests unless my friend can get up here. I sent her a text and want to talk to her. She's in medical school and can be busy."

"I'm sure she's not too busy for your wedding."

"How many times do you think her professors will fall for the 'my best friend is getting married' excuse? I kind of have a track record."

"Runaway bride," Margaret said. "I saw the article."

"You know it isn't true. I didn't leave Van. I left Phillip." I wrapped my arms around my midsection. "I was so confused as to why Van would push to marry at my parents'. It felt wrong." I exhaled. "It was wrong. Once Van caught up and found me at my parents' house, we both left. Neither one of us wanted to get married in Chicago or at my parents'."

Margaret shook her head. "I never take any of the news flashes about Donovan to heart."

"Good."

Margaret and I walked together back to the private living room and the remaining boxes and totes.

"What do we have left?" she asked.

"Mostly books, journals, and trinkets. I think we can

stack the boxes and totes, and I'll deal with them a little at a time."

"Are you sure?"

"Yes. I want to try to call Vicki again."

Margaret reached for my arm. "Let me clean the suite where you were staying. That way if your friend can make it, the room's ready. If there are others, it won't take much to make the other rooms presentable."

I wasn't sure what made me think about it. "What is on the third floor?" Before she answered, I added, "I've looked up there. It just seems empty."

Margaret feigned a smile. "A single man with too much space. I think he forgets it's even there. I haven't been up there in years." She took a breath. "Now, I'll get to your old suite."

"You've already done so much."

"Tell me," she said, tilting her head, "do you have anything planned for next Saturday? What about the marriage license?"

"Nothing planned, not even a Wisconsin license. There is one for Illinois..."

"Did you know that Wisconsin has a six-day waiting period?"

"Shit." I looked at my watch. "Today's Friday. Do you know when the courthouse closes?"

"Honestly, I bet Donovan can get an exemption."

She was probably right that he could. However, in my head, "simple" meant by the rules and without fanfare, no string pulling and no calls to make sure an old license was still valid.

"Maybe we have time," I said, opening one of the boxes we just stacked. "My birth certificate is in one of these."

She reached for another box. "Will I know it? Is there an envelope?"

"It's in a folder with my passport. I was supposed to be on my way back from Europe right now."

"A quick afternoon trip to Ashland's courthouse is almost as fun."

I pulled the folder out from the box I'd recently closed. "Here it is."

"Go," she said. "Tell your fiancé that you need to get to town."

When I opened the bedroom door, I paused. "Thank you, Margaret, for everything."

"Is the wedding a secret, or can I tell my mother?"

"Since she's invited, you can tell her."

"What about food and decorations?"

I shook my head. "Nothing planned. I want it simple."

"Let me rephrase," she said with a grin. "Would you give Mom and I the honor of preparing the cabin and some refreshments?"

"Isn't your mom busy with cooking for us and the new security team?"

"Is she busy? Yes, and she loves to feel useful."

"Okay, then yes. Thank you."

"Go," she said, "the courthouse closes at four-thirty."

I stopped after a few steps in the hallway and ran back to the closet. "Boots. I need my boots."

Margaret laughed.

"I know, I'm scattered."

"No, Julia. You're the breath of fresh air Donovan and this house needed."

I reached for her hand. "Thank you."

With my birth certificate and passport in hand and my feet covered in boots, I hurried down the stairs toward Van's office.

Chapter 19

Van

Julia's smile shone through the window of my truck as I closed the door behind her and walked around to the driver's side. Despite the cold air and waning sunlight, Ashland was alive with people and cars. The courthouse parking lot was still relatively full. A man who worked at the coffee shop waved as he got into his car. Before I was barely seated, Julia leaned across the seat, kissing my cheek.

"We made it," she said as the engine roared to life.

"We did." We'd made it in time to the courthouse. There was little doubt I could have gotten us an exemption, and with the logjam of work I left behind, I should have insisted we wait until next week. But after listening to the voicemail Phillip left Connie, Julia's arrival to my office door was the distraction I couldn't resist.

And her damn smile beaming my direction.

"I wonder why they make you wait six days," Julia mused as I drove the truck back toward the house and away from town. Her blue eyes widened. "You don't think they could decide not to issue the license because I have other licenses in Illinois, do you?"

"You have no weddings, only the purchase of the licenses."

"How did Phillip get a license for us in Illinois?" she asked. "Skylar and I applied together. You and I just applied together. We needed our birth certificates. I have mine and you have yours. I didn't go with anyone to apply for the Illinois license. I don't understand how they could have applied."

The setting sun was below the trees, causing a strobing effect as the heater blew warm air into the cab of the truck.

"That's a good question."

"I have another good question," Julia said as I drove us toward home.

"Do I have a good answer?"

"I don't know. Is your work done for the day? Do we need to go back home?"

I grinned as I turned her way, my gaze narrowing. "That was the plan. What are you thinking, beautiful?"

"I was talking to Margaret about the wedding next weekend...and it got me thinking about the cabin." She shrugged. "I miss it."

"You miss the cabin." I looked at the outside temperature on the dashboard. "It's only twenty-two degrees. I know this area well enough to know it will drop even colder during the night."

It wasn't that I didn't see the merit in Julia's idea. It

was more about keeping her at the big house with the increased security. A cabin without electricity wasn't exactly easy to equip with sensors and cameras.

A sexy shimmer shone in her blue eyes. "Hmm. I wonder how we could keep warm."

Fuck.

I knew exactly how we could keep warm.

"Security—"

Julia reached for my arm. "Van, I promise to get used to having them around, but didn't you say that Phillip is still in Chicago? You said your PI saw him."

I had told her about my conversation with Rob and the picture of Logan and Phillip at the hotel restaurant.

"Yes, I did," I said. "We still don't know if someone else has your phone." I'd been giving credence to the idea that Phillip and Logan weren't working alone. Before I worried Julia with that idea, I wanted proof.

"My dad promised to have my old number disconnected today. It probably already is."

While I was happy no more false messages could be sent, part of me wanted to keep tracking the phone.

Julia squeezed my coat sleeve. "Mrs. Mayhand had only begun the cooking when we left. She said she'll be at the house until late this evening. She was busy this morning cooking at the guesthouse." She sighed. "After all we went through yesterday, I'd love for it to be the two of us tonight, no security, no one cooking. Just us."

"If we want to go to the cabin, I should tell Michael.

Hell, I'll need to give him directions to find the cabin's location."

"Having Michael there isn't us alone."

"Not to stay. He should know where we are."

"If no one can find the cabin, it must be safe," Julia reasoned.

"People can find the cabin if they know where they're looking."

Did Phillip know the location? A lot had changed on my property since he was last here, or at least, the last time I knew he was here.

"Then it's settled."

I lifted my brow. "What is?"

"We're taking a break from reality—we've had enough lately. Besides, we should clean up the tree and decorations from Christmas before Margaret and Paula go out there to decorate for the wedding."

The darkening sky and the mention of Mrs. Mayhand reminded me that I'd only had a small lunch. "What about dinner?"

"Soup and nectarines?"

"No nectarines in the truck or cabin. I have an idea. We can drive up to Bayfield, get a dinner to go and some muffins from the bakery for the morning. Then we can head to the cabin."

Julia let out a long breath as she laid her head against the seat. "Thank you."

It was my turn to reach out. Laying my hand on her

thigh, I squeezed. "I'll tell you again, I'm sorry for not letting you know about Phillip."

When she turned, her expression had changed. Gone was the smile from seconds before.

"What's the matter?" I asked.

"I'm trying not to think about yesterday, but I can't help it."

"They didn't win, Julia. We did. Don't spend time thinking about someone who doesn't deserve your attention."

"My thoughts aren't about what happened. I keep thinking about what didn't happen," she said.

My grip of the steering wheel tightened. Those weren't thoughts I wanted Julia to ponder; nevertheless, she was.

She went on, "What happened with Phillip surfacing and the fiasco at my parents' was a disruption, but Van, it could have been so much more. Maybe we're wrong about the goal."

"What do you mean?"

"I mean that while the goal could have been to make me change my mind about you, what if...what if I hadn't known something was wrong? What if I'd gone along with the wedding all the way, married him? What if he hadn't walked out on me and then...he'd done more than kiss me? What if he'd...?"

I pulled the truck to the side of the road as the wheels crunched over the packed snow. After putting the truck in park, I leaned closer, reaching for Julia's hands. "I won't let him near you ever again. You have my word."

Her eyes glistened with unshed tears as she nodded.

"If he had touched you in any other way, I'd kill him."

Julia's eyes blinked rapidly, causing a lone tear to escape. She quickly wiped it away. "No, Van. If you did that, I'd lose you too. He didn't. It's that with the more time that passes, the less relieved I am that we made it away, and the more I question the what-ifs."

"We just applied for our *real* marriage license," I reminded her. "No one can stop us now. I know I just agreed to a night without security, but that doesn't mean we're getting rid of them. You have to know that keeping you safe is my number-one priority."

She nodded. "I know."

The headlights of another car reflected in the rearview mirror as we kissed. The car slowed as it drove past us before speeding up again.

"Is that car familiar?" she asked. "Did you know them?"

"No. Why?"

Julia shook her head. "It was odd how they slowed."

"The conditions aren't great out here. Maybe they were checking to be sure we were all right and saw our exhaust and figured we were." When Julia didn't respond, I asked, "Did you see the driver?"

"No, I'm not even sure of the color of the car. It's getting dark." She shook her head. "I think all your warnings and what happened yesterday has messed with me." She took a deep breath. "Let's get dinner and then we can forget about reality."

"I promise to take your mind off everything but us."

"I like that promise."

"Then consider it made," I said. "First, I'll call Michael and tell him our plans before we're without a signal."

Less than an hour later, with a dinner, breakfast, and a few extras, I pulled the truck onto the nearly hidden road leading up to the cabin. Our headlights sent bright LED beams through the darkness and the trees and foliage beyond the lane until the cabin came into view.

With the dark sky and tall trees, it was easy to miss the plume of smoke. My attention was on a glow coming from within. It was as I opened the truck door that the scent of burning wood added to my unease. My gaze met Julia's. "Stay in the truck and lock the doors."

"Why?"

My focus went to the tire tracks in the packed snow and ice. Looking around, I saw no signs of another car or a person. But if there was a fire...

"Let me check the cabin first."

"No, Van. I don't want to be out here alone."

"Lock the doors," I demanded as I shut the door.

It was hard to decipher if I was seeing fresh or old tire tracks and shoe prints. The last big snow we'd had was before we left for Chicago. Since then the temperatures had plummeted. Sunshine could melt snow, even in the cold, enough for tracks to morph and become hard as ice.

I turned back at the slamming of the truck door. Julia was out of the truck, her hands in her coat pockets and hat on her head as she hurried my way. When my gaze met Julia's, I scowled. "You're not in the truck."

"Is that smoke? Is the fireplace going? Who's inside?"

"That's what I was about to find out."

Her head moved back and forth as she reached out and grabbed my arm. "I changed my mind. Let's go home."

"Maybe Michael came here, checked out the cabin for us and started a fire."

"Call him. Oh, you can't." She tugged me toward the truck. "What if it's someone else?"

"No one is on our property, no one who doesn't belong."

My reassurance was more to ease her mind. This part of the property wasn't under surveillance. The cold air nipped at my face as my skin warmed from within, precipitated by my need to be sure. Our boots crunched the snow and ice as we made it closer to the cabin door.

"Please, Van. What if someone is in there?"

Chapter 20

Julia

"Please, let's go home," I said again, unable to ignore the growing sense of dread. Its dark tentacles stretched beneath my skin. "You can make me forget about everything there. I know you can."

"This is wrong, Julia. You shouldn't be afraid here. Don't let anyone have that kind of control."

"We'll come back tomorrow...when it's light."

I followed Van's lead, lifting my chin and peering up at the light gray smoke contrasting the black velvet sky as fright gave way to concern. "The Christmas tree is in there. It's probably all dried out by now. A fire shouldn't be left burning."

Van kissed my forehead. "Go back to the truck."

"What if there's someone with a gun, maybe a hunter or someone worse?"

"There's no car or truck." He looked around the side of the cabin. "Not even a snowmobile. No one is here."

If it weren't for the confirmation of the fire within, I would insist we head back to the house. I saw the interior in my mind's eye—wooden furniture, blankets, and throw rugs. With the addition of our dried-out tree, the cabin was a tinderbox ready to ignite.

I couldn't fathom why Michael would leave a fire unattended.

Van turned the doorknob and pushed the door inward.

Tepid air met us as we stepped inside.

I let out the breath I was holding as we both scanned the one room, finding we were alone. "Where's the tree?" I asked.

As my eyes adjusted to the firelight, I walked to where we'd had the tree set up. Spinning around, I took in the room from all directions. The tree wasn't only gone, there was no sign of needles or decorations. My boots tapped on the wood floor of the kitchen area. It too was without pine needles. When I turned, Van was down on his haunches, inspecting the fire within the hearth.

"The fire isn't new," he said. "It's been burning for a while. The grate is hot as if the fire has been burning for hours or days."

He pointed to the rack that holds firewood. I recalled that Van had filled it with logs for our Christmas celebration. Since we decided to head back to the house early, there should be a larger stack.

"Wasn't there more wood?" I asked.

"That's what I was thinking."

Walking deeper into the kitchen, I noticed one of

the mugs from the pegs was in the sink with a spoon. "Van, someone has been here, and I don't think it was Michael."

He came closer, reaching for the handle to the pump, lifting it up and pushing it down. After two such movements, the water began to flow. "It's been primed."

"Who would use your cabin? Who would clean it?" I met his green gaze and his stern expression. "Margaret? She didn't mention it."

Van shook his head. "Margaret doesn't come out here without permission. This is my retreat."

"It looks like it's someone else's too."

I walked over to the bed. The quilt was pulled up like it had been when we left. I gripped the hem of the covers and pulled them down. "Shit."

Van was beside me. "What?"

"Look at the pillow. It's dented."

"We spent the night—"

"No," I interrupted. "We changed the sheets before we left. Remember?"

Going back to the kitchen, Van took a pan from below the counter and filled it with water from the pump.

"I thought you said that needed to be boiled."

"We're not staying, and we're not drinking it. I'm going to use this to douse the fire."

The logs sizzled and flames hissed as he poured the water. Smoke and steam escaped the hearth. Van returned to the sink. With the fire extinguished, the

cabin was now in near darkness. Watching his silhou-
ette, he filled the pan once again.

I wrapped my arms around my midsection as he
repeated the quenching of the coals below the grate.
Setting the pan on the hearth, Van took out his phone
and turned on the flashlight.

"Julia, look."

Avoiding the sparse furniture, I went to him,
crouching down at his side. "What?"

Handing me the phone and telling me to keep it
pointed at the ashes, Van took an iron poker and
pushed some ashes from the side of the fireplace. The
charred glass reflected the flashlight's beam.

"What is it?"

"I think our decorations." He fluffed the ashes,
revealing the remaining inches of a strand of beads.

"Who would burn our tree and our decorations?"

Van stood, put the poker back in its holder, and
reached for my hand. "Come on. Now we're leaving."

"Our wedding?" I said, letting his hand encase
mine.

"I'll have Jonathon bring Michael and Albert here
tomorrow. Let them figure out how to secure the
cabin."

"Shouldn't we call the police? I mean there's DNA
on the cup and spoon, right?"

"It could have been a hunter who got lost. Nothing
appears stolen."

"Our tree and the decorations were burned," I

reminded him, my volume increasing. "What if this was Phillip?"

"I told you, he's in Chicago and has been for a couple of days."

On the nights we'd stayed in the cabin, the burning fire had gone out while we slept. That meant that whoever built this fire tended to it in the last few hours. "I'm scared."

Van's arms encircled me, pulling me against him. "We're going home where I promise to take your mind off everything."

Closing my eyes, I let my forehead fall to his wide chest. "This is our special place." My words were muffled by the bulk of his coat.

"Anyplace with you is special."

When I looked up, I saw something out of the corner of my eye. Turning, I stared at the windowpanes. "I think I saw something or someone."

Taking my hand, Van walked to the window and stared.

"I don't see anything or anyone."

"What about tracks in the snow?" I tried to look beyond the glass. With no light within, we had an unob-structed albeit muted view of trees and snow. "Maybe I'm going crazy."

"No, beautiful. The only thing crazy about you is how crazy in love I am with you."

Despite my clothes and coat, a chill scattered over my flesh, causing me to shiver. "Let's go home."

Outside, the wind howled as Van pulled the door to the cabin shut.

"Aren't you going to lock it?"

"The single lock can be engaged only from the inside." He placed his hand in the small of my back. "I'll have Jonathon change that tomorrow."

As we walked to the truck, I scanned as far as I could see as I also listened for noises in the distance. Once we were both back in the truck and the warm air was flowing, Van reached for my hand. "I'm sorry, Julia. It could be a transient person who just happened onto the cabin. It's been very cold and maybe they needed a place to stay."

"Do you really believe that? Has it happened before?"

"I don't know," he said as he turned the truck around and headed toward the lane. "I don't come out here as much in the winter. It could have happened before without me being aware."

"We didn't check the outhouse," I said as we drove farther from the cabin.

We rode in silence down the lane until we made it to the main road. A few miles more and we came to the newly closed gate. After entering the code, the gate allowed us entry. My attention was out into the trees as the truck's headlights illuminated the wilderness.

The golden hue of the house subdued the forest. In our driveway were two vehicles.

"Albert and Mrs. Mayhand," Van answered my unspoken question.

It was no secret that the incident in Chicago was weighing on both of us.

However, tonight's discovery was different. I couldn't compartmentalize it to a city seven hours away. Someone had been within the confines of our snow globe. I swallowed the mix of emotions—fear, disappointment, unease—as Van pulled his truck into the large garage.

I turned to Van in question.

The bright light from the ceiling highlighted his tense features, letting me know I wasn't alone in my thoughts. He pulled out his phone and peered down at the screen.

"The sensors show a person in the kitchen and another in the living room. Mrs. Mayhand and Albert."

I nodded. "No one else."

Van shook his head. "No one. The new heat sensors show the entire floor plan."

"Even the third floor?"

Van's gaze narrowed. "Why would you ask that?"

"That room is empty and never used."

"It isn't equipped yet, but I'll have Jonathon get on it." He reached for my hand. "Our dinner is probably cold."

"I'm not hungry."

"I know how to build up your appetite."

When I didn't reply, Van released my hand and

wrapped his arms around me. "I won't let you out of my sight."

Van closed the garage door as we made our way down the breezeway toward the kitchen doorway. Hanging our coats in the mudroom, I opened the door. I'd been wrong about not wanting to come home to Paula's cooking.

The bright kitchen was welcoming, filled with lights and delicious aromas. Her tired smile beamed as we entered.

"Congratulations. I just heard we have a wedding to plan."

Her enthusiasm was exactly what I needed to chip away at the concoction of emotions stifling our snow globe.

"The wedding is on," I said, smiling up at Van. "The location is still under consideration."

"Peggy," Paula said, using her daughter's nickname, "and I have been talking about the cabin. We have ideas."

"Did Margaret go out there?" Van asked.

Paula shook her head. "No. We were going to check with you and go tomorrow." When neither of us responded, her gaze narrowed, bringing small lines to the side of her eyes. "Is something wrong?"

"No," Van said, squeezing my hand. "Stay with Mrs. Mayhand. I need to speak to Albert."

Pulling out one of the stools from the counter, I climbed up as Van disappeared beyond the living room.

With my hands clasped on the counter, I let my chin fall toward my chest as I tried to think of anything and nothing.

"Child, are you okay?"

I shook my head, suddenly fighting tears I didn't know were ready to flow.

Paula turned down whatever was on the stove and came around the counter. Before I knew it, her hand was covering mine and her face was close. I stared into her brown eyes. "I'm sorry," I said.

Paula shook her head slowly. "Apologies aren't necessary. What can I get you?"

"A new snow globe."

Her face tilted. "He's a complicated man, Julia. Complicated men need love too."

I scoffed as I wiped away the tears. "It's not him. I do love him."

"Peggy told me what happened in Chicago. Take some time, this weekend, to try to forget about it. Concentrate on the two of you. Next week, you can pick up the fight."

"We went to the cabin," I confessed. "I wanted to spend the night there." I shook my head. "There was a fire in the fireplace and dishes in the sink."

Paula stood straighter, her petite form going stiff.

"Tell me what you're thinking," I said.

She feigned a grin. "We've told Mr. Sherman to lock that place. Who knows who decided to make it their temporary home."

"You've told him?"

"Bruce did. I think Jonathon has too."

"Why didn't he?"

"I don't know the reason. I have my suspicion."

"I'm listening," I said.

"As I said, Mr. Sherman is complicated. He's a shrewd businessman. If I were to believe all the stories, well, some would say he's heartless." Her head shook as she grinned. "That may be true. But there's more to him than meets the eye."

I nodded.

"The cabin and the guesthouse were two of the original buildings on this property before Mr. Sherman purchased it. The cabin is...well, you've seen it. It's primitive."

"Yes."

"When he is in a mood, he goes out there. It's his haven."

"Why hasn't he kept it locked?"

"My suspicion is that by keeping it open, he has it available for those in need. He's become an icon in the business world, yet there's a part of him that is kind-hearted and generous. The cabin is only one example of that."

I let her words sink in. "Maybe you're right. After what happened in Chicago, my nerves are stretched to their limit. Thinking about someone in the cabin was the final straw." I took a deep breath. "Van said he'll have Jonathon secure the door tomorrow. Maybe I should tell him not to worry about it."

Paula's grin broadened. "No, child. He knows you are upset. Men like him are all about fixing problems. You are his priority. Think about those men he just hired. Before you, he wouldn't welcome people into his world. Now he has."

"I don't want to change who Van is. I love him the way I found him, or he found me."

"Change isn't always bad. If you will listen to an old lady's advice, I say talk about it. Don't hold back. Be honest. And when he's honest with you, accept what he says. Sometimes truth is difficult to say and hear, but it's the only element that can't be ignored."

"Julia."

We both turned toward Van's voice.

I reached for Paula's slender shoulders and gave her a quick hug. "Thank you."

"You two should eat," she said.

Getting down from the tall stool, I reached for the bag we'd placed on the table and lifted it. "It won't be as good as your cooking, but we picked up something in Bayfield."

"I'll be out of here in another hour."

As I reached for Van's hand, he replied to Paula, "Let Albert know when you're leaving. The doors are currently monitored. He'll see you to your car."

21

Van

With Julia's hand in mine, my thoughts were uncharacteristically distracted. Instead of thinking about the beauty at my side, I was rethinking my conversation with Albert. I wanted to be as open as I could with Julia without scaring her more than she already was.

The reality was that we were all concerned about the cabin. It was more than that. There were also red flags at the guesthouse.

Jonathon said that when he opened the house, things seemed out of place. Nothing overt. Nothing to scream that there had been intruders. While seventy-plus acres wasn't massive, it was too much land to keep fully monitored. Having the two men staying at the guesthouse should scare off any local kids looking for a place to fool around. That was Jonathon's thought. He said the options in and around Ashland for teenagers were limited. It wasn't unusual for them to break into seasonal homes and hang out. Their intent wasn't malicious as much as it was for a place to do whatever it was they wanted to do.

As I opened the door to our suite, Julia released my hand, and wrapping her arms around herself, she sighed. "Can we stay locked in these rooms?"

"We can do whatever you want." I tried for humor. "Of course, if we do that, you may have to tell the state patrol I have you held captive."

Coming closer, she wrapped her arms around my torso and laid her cheek against my chest. "Hold me captive." Her soft blue stare looked up through her lashes. "Right here."

Julia had no idea how much I wanted that, how I wanted to sever her connection to the outside world, take away her distractions, and keep her all to myself.

Closing her eyes and lowering her chin, her words were muffled against my shirt. "I'm worn out."

With my thumb and forefinger, I lifted her chin until her stunning blue orbs were fixed on my gaze. "Let me take care of you."

Her eyelids fluttered. "Sleeping wrapped in your arms for the next month sounds like the answer."

"First things first." I turned the small lever in the doorknob, locking the door from the suite to the hallway. "You're now captive. My prisoner to do with what I want."

"You can't scare me, Van. I've yet to find anything you want not to my approval."

Taking her hand, I led Julia into the attached bathroom.

"What is your plan, Mr. Sherman?"

"My plan is for you to relax, to forget about anything beyond these walls, and rest, knowing you're safe and loved."

As I reached for the hem of Julia's sweater, she lifted her arms, allowing me to pull the soft top over her head. Without a word, she grinned my direction, patiently waiting for my next move.

"I love undressing you." My gaze locked on the way her camisole tented over her hardening nipples. "You're a treasure, Julia. I'm so fucking lucky to have found you."

Her arms came up and around my neck. "I'm glad you found me."

"I don't want you to regret that, ever."

"I don't. There's us and the world. I won't give up on one because of the other."

Fuck the world and everyone else in it.

Crouching down, I closed the drain and turned on the water in the bathtub.

As the large tub began to fill, I tested the water. Standing, I brushed Julia's lips with mine. Lifting her by the waist, I sat her on the edge of the wide vanity and tended to her socks, before tugging down her slacks. The pile of clothes on the floor grew as the bathroom warmed and the bathtub filled.

With her wearing only the camisole and panties, I took a step back. My lips curled as her cheeks blushed with pink. "You're fucking gorgeous. I want you to know that I see how stunning you are every time I look at you. Never doubt that I'm awed by you."

"I'm feeling underdressed."

"No, beautiful. You're still overdressed."

As I took a step closer, Julia's fingers went to the buttons on my shirt. The suit coat and tie were lost long ago.

"If the plan is for me to get in that giant bathtub," she said with a grin, "I don't want to get in alone."

My hands ached to touch her as she slowly undid the buttons. One by one she loosened their grip, leaned forward, and left a kiss on my chest. It wasn't until she'd pushed the material over my shoulders that I stepped between her knees and lifted the camisole over her head. Julia's long blond hair cascaded down her back as her round globes heaved with a deep breath and goose bumps scattered over her skin. She leaned back, pressing her pert breasts toward me and putting her weight on her back-stretched arms.

From where I stood, I saw her soft curves before me and her slender shoulders and spine in the reflection. Lifting her hair, my lips met her neck as I teased her sensitive skin behind her ear. Slowly, I lowered myself as my kisses rained over her collarbone and down to each breast.

Her nipples hardened as I sucked and nipped, dividing my attention between the two as the water continued to flow. Unable to keep my hands to myself, my touch roamed over her body, her arms and down her ribcage. Over her hips and her thighs, my fingers caressed. It was as if the more of her I touched, the more I wanted.

Each contact confirmed her presence, her realness, and her safety.

Before long, steam obscured our reflections.

I turned off the water and shed my shoes, socks, and pants, letting them join Julia's clothes on the tile floor. Wearing only my boxer briefs, I secured the hem of her panties and taking a step back, tugged the lace down her shapely legs. For longer than I intended, my gaze was glued to her perfect pink pussy. With each second, my cock hardened while simultaneously, I pushed away the unexpected rage brewing within me.

If I hadn't found Julia when I did, if I'd been an hour later...Her confession in the truck, thinking about what-ifs. My grip of her thighs increased as my fingers held tight.

"Van," Julia said, lifting my chin and refocusing my vision on her. "Stay with me."

My nostrils flared at the realization she was right. I'd left our bubble; my thoughts had filled with my determination to destruction. I'd make Phillip and the Butlers pay for what they did.

But not Julia.

She was innocent.

Cupping the bulge of my hardened cock beneath my boxers, I refocused. "Oh, I'm with you. You're the only one who makes me painfully hard."

Julia scooted from the counter, her feet landing on the tile seconds before she reached for my boxers, pulling them down, and freeing my hard cock. It sprang to life as I kicked the silky material away.

As I reached for her hand, Julia fell to her knees. Her lashes veiled her seductive blue stare as she peered up at me a millisecond before her lips opened and she teased the head of my cock.

"Fuck."

My grip of the vanity intensified as Julia's head bobbed up and down, her tongue and lips giving attention to my hard rod as her fingers rolled my heavy balls. Her actions sent sensations to my scalp and down to my toes. My feet spread apart as my fingers splayed over her hair.

Julia teased and tormented as her tongue swirled around the tip of my cock and her fingers moved up and down the thickened appendage. Taking only an inch at a time, she took me between her lips, each move taking me deeper over her tongue and deeper still until she had me near the back of her throat.

Her breaths came in quick gusts as she increased her pace.

She was fucking gorgeous on her knees.

A wave of impending release overtook me as I held Julia's head in place, thrusting faster and deeper. The frustrations of the unknown and the anger at the known all came together, propelling me as the tension built.

"Fuck," I growled, realizing what I was doing.

I took a step back.

Julia deserved better than me using her in this way.

Her grasp of my thighs tightened, refusing to take the out I was offering.

"Fuck, I'm going to come."

My announcement didn't slow her. The suction built as she bobbed her head faster.

Dark spots danced in the bright lights as my body tensed. I called out her name in a roar. Over and over, her lips moved up and down as she swallowed, taking all of me and all I had to give.

Curses and murmurs filled the humid air as I closed my eyes and savored my release.

When my eyes opened, I offered Julia my hand, helping her stand and taking in her swollen lips and the gleam in her eyes. "Fuck, that was..." I cupped her cheek with my palm. "You're supposed to let me take care of you."

"You said I was supposed to stay focused on us. I was."

My grin returned.

"We're not done," she said.

"No, beautiful. We're not done."

The water sloshed as we settled in the warm bath. With her hair now piled high, Julia's head laid against my chest. Cupping the water, I rained it over her shoulders. Beneath the surface, my touch wandered over her thighs and between her legs.

Julia's back arched against me as I circled her clit. My lips kissed her neck as my fingers plunged into her tight, warm pussy. Sliding in and out, my fingers covered with her essence as I continued teasing and taunting.

Her fingers gripped my knees as soft moans and whimpers filled the air.

"That's it," I coaxed.

Tighter, I wound her. Like an antique toy, I'd bring her to the brink and let her settle. My goal was near as I followed through until spasms overtook her body and she cried out. When she collapsed against me, her heart pounded as she curled toward me.

"That was..."

It was all-encompassing.

It centered her thoughts.

It had her thinking only about us.

"It was beautiful," I said. "I could watch you come for hours."

Slowly spinning, Julia craned her neck as her eyes met mine. "Hours?"

"Days, weeks, months, and years."

"If your goal was to relax me, you did it," she said

with a beautiful grin. "If your goal is to make me come again, I think your work is cut out for you."

"Is that a challenge?"

"Are you up for it?"

I kissed her pink lips. "I'm pretty sure you know I am."

Chapter 22

Julia

Van handed me the wine glass he'd just refilled as a fire crackled in the fireplace before us. We'd spent the weekend isolated in the master bedroom suite and as Sunday came to a close, I wanted to rewrite the calendar, rearrange the days, and suspend the rotation of the earth. In the span of forty-eight hours, I'd officially become a recluse.

Leaving the world behind wasn't anything like I thought it would be.

It was the opposite.

Fulfilling, comforting, and secure.

"Talk to me, beautiful," Van said, teasing my sock-covered toes from the blanket I had over me.

Taking a sip of the semi-sweet rosé, I turned from the orange flames to Van's face, scanning his features from his dark mane to his protruding brow, high cheek-bones, firm lips, and chiseled jawline. "What if I don't want to talk? I just want to soak up this time, just the two of us."

"You haven't asked about the cabin."

I hadn't.

Shaking my head, I set the wine glass on a nearby table.

"It's secure," he said. "The door has a lock. The windows are secured. No one is getting in without a key."

"I don't think I've asked because I want to forget that someone intruded."

"Where do you want to marry, Julia? If it isn't the cabin any longer, tell me. We can marry here in the living room, up here in our suite. Hell, we can marry out on the bay in a fishing hut. I don't care. All I care about is officially making you mine."

My gaze went to the diamond on my left hand and back to Van. "I'm pretty sure that I'm officially yours."

His smile grew as he leaned toward me, crawling over me on his hands and knees like a lion stalking its prey. It wasn't until our noses were nearly touching that his lips captured mine.

His tasted of the wine we'd been drinking as his tongue sought entrance. Palming his stubbly cheeks, I pulled him closer until his weight was over me. Wiggling beneath him, I took comfort in his presence. As if Van were my lifeline, I felt more alive when he was with me.

"Take me." It was my only request. I didn't want to think about leaving the suite or even about our impending wedding. I wanted what we had when we were here.

If Albert and Michael had been in the house since Friday night, I didn't know.

Our meals came when Van slipped away for a few minutes, leaving me alone staring at the double doors. I knew enough about mental health to know mine was on the decline.

Phillip hadn't hurt me, not physically and perhaps not emotionally as may have been his intention, and still I was plagued with the what-ifs.

What if he had?

What if I'd married him?

What if I'd turned away from Van and gone to Skylar?

I'd wake in the middle of the night, my skin dampened with perspiration and my flesh cold to the touch. Whatever or whoever I saw beyond the cabin's windows was omnipresent in my dreams, a figure, a ghost. I couldn't make out the particulars, yet I felt it—her or him. The sense that I wasn't alone even during the times Van slipped away ate at me.

I tried to talk to him about it such as Paula had recommended, but the words didn't form. My worries would add to his. I didn't want to do that to him. Whatever was happening beyond this suite was on Van's radar.

I knew it was.

His expression would sour as he read text messages. Now and then he'd slip into the small office, hiding behind the door I hadn't checked the first night. It was a miniature version of what he had downstairs. A desk with computers and a view of the forest beyond the house.

Questions came to me, but I didn't verbalize them.

In all honesty, I didn't want to know more answers.

For the past two days, I lived in our bubble, pretending our snow globe was intact. The façade soothed me. I longed to linger in the glistening flakes of the silvery snow and the golden specks within Van's gaze.

Reality wouldn't leave us as much as I wanted it to. It would be waiting on Monday morning. As our time alone dwindled away, my desire was to hold on with both hands and savor the final seconds.

A chill scattered over my skin as Van pulled the blanket to the floor and tugged my satin pajama shorts down my legs. The cold was short-lived as he settled between my legs, his hardening cock pressed against my core.

How many times had we made love since our bath on Friday night?

I'd lost count.

As we came together on the soft blanket over the sofa in front of the fire, our passion simmered like the glowing embers beneath the burning wood. The heat was there, ready to burst into flames as Van filled me. My back arched and my hips lifted, taking him in and accommodating his familiar girth. His calm rhythm created a steady cadence. The rush we'd experienced upon finding the cabin violated had settled like the snow upon the bay.

There was a diamond on my finger and a marriage license in Van's office.

We didn't need to prove our adoration to anyone.

This was our world, our globe, and our bubble.

Outside forces had threatened to shatter what we'd built.

They failed.

The only true destruction could come from within. And as Van continued to fill me, moving tenderly in and out as his lips captured mine, and the stubble of his cheeks brought my nerve endings to life, I knew without a doubt I was home and safe. For my part, when this weekend ended, I'd face the world and do my piece to reinforce what we'd built and what our future could be.

My orgasm came like the igniting of a candle.

A burst before the warmth spread and the wax melted.

I held tight to his shoulders as Van found his own release, relishing the way our bodies fit together. When he lifted his face and our eyes met, I saw the golden flecks reflecting in the firelight.

"You're insatiable," he said before his lips landed on mine. "Maybe I'm too old after all."

I palmed his cheeks. "You're perfect."

"That's you."

Momentarily, I mourned the fullness as Van and I disconnected.

Sitting up, I pulled the blanket from the floor to cover myself and asked, "What were you like when you were my age?"

Van took a deep breath and after pulling on his boxers, sat with my feet in his lap. "Driven. Ruthless. Reckless. Obsessed."

"Obsessed with Madison?" I wasn't sure what prompted the question.

"Not completely."

"No?"

"Later it was different. At twenty-four my main goal was success."

"Did you know her yet?"

His Adam's apple bobbed. "I did. We met at a coffee shop in the middle of the night. Two insomniacs not looking for anyone."

"Do you think you and she would have ended differently if you were already successful?"

His jaw clenched, a nonverbal clue that I was about out of questions. Nevertheless, I waited.

"I'm not sure she would have turned to Phillip, but I don't think in the long run we would have made it."

"May I ask why?"

His neck straightened as his green gaze went to the fire's flames. "Ambition."

"You had too much? She had too much?"

"Madison was a content person. She didn't understand my need for more, bigger, and better. She was complacent with mediocrity." Before I could respond, Van turned to me. "You aren't her, Julia. Don't ever think you are. I lived a life before you, before I found the perfect woman along the side of the road. I can't take that back or make it disappear."

"I'd never ask you to."

"Do you know where I would have found Madison if she were you?"

Pulling the blanket higher over my shoulders, I shook my head.

"In the car, probably frozen to death."

It wasn't the response I imagined. "Why?"

"Because she wouldn't have done what you did. She wouldn't have risked walking in a blizzard. She wouldn't have spoken to Wade's executive board or refused her mother like you have." He shrugged. "I don't know about her mother. Her parents died when she was young."

That bit of information filled me with a new sadness for the woman I didn't know. "That must have been hard."

"Her sister took care of her...until she couldn't."

"Until Phillip?" I asked.

Van nodded. "I'm done walking down memory lane."

Sitting forward, I reached for his hand. "Whenever you're ready for another walk, I'm here, holding your hand and walking beside you."

"I don't need memories, Julia. I want a future."

"Better than the past."

"Always better."

I gathered my strength. "Tomorrow I'll call Margaret and see if she wants to go to the cabin to discuss decorations."

"Michael—"

"He or Albert can drive, not because I'm scared but because I know you have work that you've been putting off, and I don't want you worrying."

"That won't stop me from worrying, but it will make me feel better. What about your work?"

"You mean with Wade?" I asked. It was something I'd thought about since our return. My laptop was in the bedroom, where I'd left it since my email to my dad. "Keep me updated on the stocks. Until we're married, I don't have a leg to stand on with Mom or the rest of the board. Next Monday, my focus will change."

"No honeymoon?"

"Did you want a honeymoon?" That hadn't occurred to me.

"We can plan something for when life isn't as crazy."

Retrieving my wine glass, I looked around the room, taking in the orange hue from the fire, the ornate woodwork, and shelves of books. "I'll take a mini honeymoon right here."

23

Van

Leaving Julia at the house was one of the most difficult things I'd done. Even though I'd left her asleep in our suite, I knew she wouldn't be alone. Michael and Albert's presence was one of the reasons I didn't reschedule my work to virtual for another day. The other reason was the message from Rob I'd received upon waking. It said that Phillip had an airline ticket. After a layover in Phoenix, this afternoon he'd arrive in San Antonio. Back home, safe and sound.

Had he given up?

Had Logan and Marlin abandoned their plan?

I didn't know the answers, yet I knew I wasn't done with any of them. They'd pay for what they'd done to Julia. Physically, she was fine. No, she was perfect. It was mentally and emotionally that I saw the wear. If I could take every what-if from her thoughts, I would.

My response to Rob was to follow Phillip to Texas or the ends of the earth. I wasn't taking any chances that his airline ticket was a false flag.

On my way into Ashland, I took a detour up to the cabin. While the sun hadn't fully risen, a red hue hung low in the horizon beyond the bay as I ascended the hill through the trees.

My loafers slipped on the frozen ground, now imprinted with even more tire tracks. They belonged to Jonathon and the rest of my security. It's what I told myself as I walked around the perimeter. My weight crunched through the hardened crust of the snow except where I could step into existing prints.

The path to the outhouse was still relatively clear from my shoveling on Christmas Eve.

The temperature warmed only from the loss of the outside breeze as I entered the cabin. The grate within the hearth was cold and the ashes near frozen. Step by step, I walked around the one room, opening cabinets and checking for signs of our trespasser.

No signs remained.

The dishes were back where they belonged, no longer in the sink, the bed was made with fresh sheets and blankets, and the logs in the holder were replenished. Jonathon had done all that I asked, restoring the cabin's allure. And yet the memory would remain of our visitor, at least until that person was identified.

"Fuck you," I said aloud to no one. "Fuck you for spoiling Julia's memories."

Sunrays from the lightening sky shone into the fireplace. A reflection glistened within the hearth, catching my attention. I crouched down prepared to see more remnants of our decorations. Using the poker, I freed the string of decorative beads we'd placed on the tree. It was as I reached for what remained that I began to question that they were indeed beads. Lifting the string between my fingers, I rotated the gritty globes with my fingertips.

The globes weren't melted or charred as the inexpensive decorations should have been. Closer inspection revealed small knots between each globe. With the end of the poker, I stirred the ash. Other radiant balls materialized.

"Shit," I murmured.

These weren't decorations. They were pearls, real pearls. Most of the satin string was gone, but the pearls remained.

No.

This was my imagination playing tricks with my mind.

No way would pearls be in the cabin.

Julia's what-ifs were mixing with my guilt.

I stuffed the remains of whatever it was that I'd found into the pocket of my overcoat before locking the cabin on my way out.

Concerns over the cabin fell to the wayside as Connie met me at the office with a full schedule. My first call was with Ashley from GreenSphere. Taking a seat behind my desk, I spent a few minutes reviewing the information from the Sherman and Madison IT division and also that from Jeremy regarding updated findings on GreenSphere and MMT Inc. While the two researchers hadn't come to the same conclusion regarding ownership of MMT Inc, their information overlapped in an interesting Venn diagram.

The shell company was one of multiple investors, most identities hidden through other shell companies and equity investment firms. Unlike many SPACs, GreenSphere had no large-name investors to entice venture capital. The underwriter was the only familiar name.

"Mr. Sherman, Ashley Conrad is on line one," Connie's voice came through the intercom.

Hitting the button, I commenced with a condensed version of early morning pleasantries before jumping into the meat of the conversation. "Your email said you wanted to make me an offer."

"Yes, Mr. Sherman. We're willing to offer you an opportunity to invest in GreenSphere."

"You want me to invest?" I'd been expecting an offer for my Wade Pharmaceutical stocks.

"Yes. I believe once I send you the prospectus on GreenSphere, you'll see that there is already substantial capital to help us toward our goal."

"Your goal?"

"Innovation."

"How does this relate to Wade Pharmaceutical?"

"Think beyond one company. Wade is but a small piece in a much larger puzzle. The pharmaceutical industry is on the brink of major changes. Wade is quite frankly ill-equipped and unprepared for the future."

"Then why has GreenSphere invested in Wade?"

"Because we have plans that involve combining private companies, including Wade, to create a worldwide competitor. Forty days ago, it was projected that Wade would fail within eighteen months. Your recent interest in the company, as well as the financial investment you made to stabilize the debt, has given Wade a few more months. Let's face it, Wade is on life support. You can either continue to invest in one of the last dinosaurs in pharmaceuticals or you can take that investment and add it to GreenSphere. GreenSphere will swallow Wade like the bad pill it is."

"Under those projections," I asked, "what will happen to Wade and its investors?"

"For a time, Wade will exist as a subsidiary. The investors will be offered pennies on the dollar. I suggest you unload your shares before that happens. However, if you choose to invest in GreenSphere, we will offer you current market value for your shares. You don't lose in this scenario. You free yourself from Wade while maintaining a voice in its future."

"Your goal isn't to take Wade public?"

"Our goals remain fluid, Mr. Sherman. Wade doesn't have the name recognition of larger companies. It had little to no recognition prior to your interest. Once you dissolve your investment, Wade too will dissolve."

"What about the other shareholders in Wade?"

"They have been offered a similar deal. Unfortunately, most do not have the available capital and will be left with whatever they can salvage."

"You have already offered this opportunity to the other shareholders?"

"Substantial shareholders."

That meant that the McGraths and Butlers have received this offer. "You only have five percent of the shares."

Ashley paused. "Mr. Sherman, this offer will expire soon. This is your opportunity to take part in the acquisition of not only Wade, but a number of other unsubstantial holdings."

"A merger?"

"The potential for success is not for the faint of heart. Tell me, Mr. Sherman, you haven't grown faint, have you?"

"You're asking," I clarified, "for Sherman and Madison to invest in GreenSphere."

"Depending upon your investment, you could acquire a seat on the board."

"And you want GreenSphere to take over my twenty-six percent of Wade's shares."

"Not twenty-six. No, for access to the board, Green-Sphere will take over sixty-five percent of Wade's stock."

"Sixty-five." That would include the percentage due to Julia upon our wedding. "If I say no?"

"You will be left with pennies on the dollar."

"Sixty-five is a majority holding."

"Mr. Sherman, this deal will expire a week from today."

Fuck.

Somehow, GreenSphere knew the date of our wedding and the transfer of stocks.

"Sir," she said, "please get back to us at your earliest convenience."

As I hung up the phone, I had to wonder what Logan Butler's role was in GreenSphere. If MMT financed Phillip's trip to Chicago and MMT was invested in GreenSphere, how much was it invested?

Were Logan and Marlin working together or was Logan trying to outsmart his brother?

Connie's voice interrupted my thoughts. "Mr. Sherman, your ten o'clock is waiting in the conference room."

I hit the button on the intercom. "Thank you, Connie. I'll be right there."

Chapter 24

I stared in disbelief as too many thoughts circled through my mind.

"Hi, Van."

Her voice was the one I heard in that space between wakefulness and sleep. It came to me when I least expected it. After a successful deal alone with my bourbon, it would remind me that I had no one with whom to share it. Hell, sometimes when I was intimate, I'd see her eyes staring back at me.

A fucking ghost, she haunted my thoughts.

As if it were All Hallows' Eve in the middle of the summer, the ghost became real.

Without my attending a séance and in the flesh, long blond hair, soft curves, smelling sweet, appearing innocent, and staring at me through wide open eyes, here she was.

I held tight to the doorjamb and edge of the front door, not opening the door any wider. My knuckles blanched as I tried to articulate my words. "Why are you here, Madison?"

Strands of her light hair fluttered around her face. Her emerald gaze peered out from below her lowered lashes. It had been five years since her wedding, five years since I'd visited her bridal suite. Five years since I'd been this close to her. Seeing her here, on my doorstep was fucking ecstasy and agony. It was the literal definition of the hell our Sunday school teachers talked about when we were kids.

I'd waited to hear that my visit spoiled their big day. Watching for anything from Olivia or even Phillip to acknowledge what I'd done, what we'd done. I'd even wondered if I'd hear from my parents. The news never came.

That didn't stop my own success.

Over the last five years my wealth had multiplied exponentially. I'd made a name where one never before existed. Hell, I'd been named most eligible bachelor by some stupid magazine. My face shone from magazine covers in newsstands and supermarket lines all over the fucking country. And every time Sherman and Madison's PR informed me of an impending publication, my first thought was the woman staring at me now.

Will she see it?

Will she wish she was the one with me?

Does she regret...?

"We're a long way from Texas," I said.

"Are you going to invite me in?"

The pressure built as I clenched my teeth. "What do you want?"

Her slender shoulders lifted and fell as she inhaled and exhaled. "You don't have to make this so hard."

I shook my head. "I don't know. It's fucking seven o'clock on a weeknight in the middle of the goddamned summer in Wisconsin. After five years you show the fuck up on my doorstep. Tell me how I'm making this hard."

Her neck tightened as she lifted her chin. "This isn't easy for me."

"What?" I asked again. "What are you doing that isn't easy?"

Madison's lips came together in a straight line as her green eyes glistened. "I knew Lena was wrong." Lowering her head, she turned away.

Reaching out, I grasped her arm and spun her back toward me. "Lena didn't tell me you were coming."

"I asked her not to. I...I thought maybe..."

My temples pounded with an explosion of memories, hopes...dare I admit...dreams. "Fuck." I pushed the front door inward. "Ten minutes, Madison. I'll give you that."

"You owe me more."

I didn't owe her a fucking thing.

That was my thought as she walked past me, stepping into my home, the one I'd purchased with the hope of more. I was done hoping. More didn't come because someone wanted it or wished for it. More came from hard work. It came with success and if others were trampled along the way, so be it. I fucking wiped the grime from my Italian leather shoes and moved on.

Until that fucking dream came steamrolling back.

She came back.

She showed up at my door.

Madison's eyes opened wide as she took in the interior. The house was nice, fucking nicer than what she had gotten used to having. Yes, I checked periodically. I sent a PI and I had Lena and Olivia to fill in blanks.

"Your house is beautiful, Van."

"Its days are numbered." There was another house on the property going through a remodel and expansion. As soon as it was completed, this one would be dust. "Much like your minutes. For the last time, what do you want?"

Her arms wrapped around her midsection as if she could hide behind them. Madison may be five years older than the last time I'd seen her, but she'd aged well. Her hair was still as blond and her eyes as vivid a green. At one time, I'd known every curve she had covered with the cheap sundress.

"I want to ask you a favor."

I lifted an eyebrow. "You want a favor from me?"

She nodded her head and walked farther into the house, pausing by the piano. "I miss hearing you play."

I no longer played. That didn't mean I'd get rid of the piano. I wouldn't.

When I didn't respond, Madison kept going, stepping over to the windows overlooking the bay. "You always said you'd get away from the city."

"Apparently, I wasn't worth the wait."

Madison spun my direction. "You're not being fair."

Fair.

What the fuck was fair about her coming to me with that pitiful ring on her finger?

"You're still married." It wasn't really a question.

Madison nodded. "Lip won't ask you...but he's had problems...since Sherman Brothers."

I stood taller. "Are you asking for me to give Lip a job?"

"No, he wouldn't take it."

"Do you want a job?"

She slowly shook her head. "No, I want something else."

"Fuck, Madison, say it and get out. My answer is to go back to your husband. You want a favor from me, bring me divorce papers. Phillip may have gotten my sloppy seconds, but I'm sure as fuck not taking his."

"He's working," she spoke fast, her words overlapping, "but it doesn't pay that well. He deserves more. All I've ever wanted was to be happy. I was hoping that maybe..."

"A loan. A gift. Help me out here. Ask your sister. She can spot you a few hundred grand."

"I don't want money, Van, and Lena can't help me, not like you can."

I had no fucking clue where this conversation was going. "Your time is about up."

"Lip...Phillip doesn't know I'm here." She turned back to the window, showing me her round ass.

"Where does he think you are?"

"Visiting Lena."

"Lena knows you're here." I wasn't asking.

"She knows to say I'm with her." Madison spun toward me; her green stare focused on mine. "I don't usually lie to him."

"Usually? You just lie to him when it's about me."

"This isn't about you, Van. It's about Lip. He's been stressed. The bills and expenses. I mean, I get it. His parents...*your* parents," she corrected, "can't help. They have their own problems. You know that."

I did.

I owned their collective failure.

It should make me feel like shit.

It didn't.

"Anyway," she hummed when I didn't take the bait. "I think what we need...well, he doesn't know I've tried, but I have for a long time and still..."

My head was about to split wide open at her fucking puzzle. I eyed the decanter of bourbon, ready to down a few fingers. "You know, Madison, I fucking hate games."

"Really? You sure as hell played one at my wedding."

It was the first time she or anyone had acknowledged what we'd done, and true to form, I felt no regret.

"How did it feel walking down the aisle with my come on your thighs?"

Her shoulders slumped. "Fuck you, Van."

I felt the tips of my lips rise. "Is that what you want? What are you saying, Lip's stressed and can't get it up? You came here to be fucked."

"No. I want a baby."

There were few moments in my life I could say I was speechless, but this was without a doubt one of them. As the smoke of her explosive statement settled, words began to form. "You're living in a hovel with a man who can't keep a job. You don't work and you want a kid."

"Don't you see? A child will show Lip that he has purpose."

The proverbial pieces of the puzzle were dropping into place.

"You think I'll fuck you?" Despite my better sense, my statement did come out as a question.

"No." She lifted her hand. "Lip would never approve."

"No shit."

"I thought maybe in vitro. You know...you supply the..."

"Why aren't you having this conversation with him?"

"Because he...don't you understand how upsetting it would be for him to realize that he can't."

"Can't get it up. There are little blue pills for that."

"It's not that. He can't produce a child."

"Do you know that?" I asked.

"I know that in the last five years, I've never been on birth control."

"Maybe you don't fuck enough." This conversation was bordering on the absurd. "Maybe it's genetic. I don't exactly have a litter of kids."

Madison's voice lowered. "You can. I know you can."

My fingers curled into fists as my nostrils flared. "What the fuck did you say?"

Her eyes widened as she took a step away. "Van, don't be mad."

Mad.

Mad wasn't even close to the emotion I felt.

"What the fuck did you say?" I repeated louder than before. "How do you know I can?"

"I was pregnant."

Pregnant.

Madison was pregnant.

"When?"

"When I went to Texas. I didn't...you didn't...we weren't ready. Lena would have been upset..."

In two strides I was upon her, my hands gripping her shoulders. "What did you do, Madison?"

She lifted her chin. "I did what was right for *me*." She took a breath. "Lip doesn't know."

"Who knew?"

"Olivia. It was why she invited me down to Texas. She said she'd help."

Letting go of her, I pushed away. Madison stepped

backward, her shoulders colliding against the windows. "Van, I'm sorry. I want that baby now."

"Well, it doesn't work like that."

"It can." She reached into her purse and pulled out a small bag. "I got this from the doctor's office. You just need to ejaculate..."

"Get the fuck out, Madison."

"Please, Van. You're my only hope. We can't afford in vitro in the traditional sense. Lip is too proud to face the truth. I mean, you two are...similar."

It was my turn to take a step back.

Maybe I wasn't thinking straight.

Madison was presenting me with the ultimate fuck-you to my brother. Would I really pass it up? I took a deep breath. "I'll think about it."

"You will?"

I softened my tone.

I'd approach this as a business negotiation. Half of what was heard was tone, not words. I softened mine. "How's your painting going?"

Her brow furrowed. "My what?"

"Your painting. You were going to be a famous artist."

"Things change."

"Stay here," I offered. "Stay here in this house and paint. We can fucking burn the paintings if you want, but I'm not jacking off in a test tube. If you want my sperm, you'll have to get it the old-fashioned way."

She shook her head.

"What's the matter? You afraid you'll realize what a loser you married."

"Van, don't."

I walked to the front door and opened it. "Go, Madison. You were the one who came to me. I'm sure as shit not fucking you against your will."

"It didn't stop you on my wedding day."

I shook my head. "Good try. You lifted your dress and spread your legs for me."

"I thought…"

"Did you? Or have you justified what we did by lying to yourself." My lips came together. "Now that I think about it and really look at you, you're a bit pathetic. Maybe I couldn't get it up for you either."

"How long?" Her gaze stayed fixed on me as she came closer. "How long, Van? How long do I need to stay?"

"Long enough to get a positive test."

"And when I do, you'll let me go. No claims on the kid."

"You're agreeing to my terms?"

"You'll let me go."

I pushed the door closed so hard that the slam reverberated through the house, rattling the front windows. I took a step toward her. "I've learned a few things over the years. I don't get into negotiations unless I'll reap the benefits."

"The kid won't be yours."

"So why would I do this?"

Madison's breasts moved as her breathing quickened. "For me. You can have me for a while."

I scoffed. "Maybe you're no longer worth the effort."

She lifted her chin. "You don't have to be so cruel."

"It appears I have all the cards in this game, or all the sperm." I grinned as I reached for the button of my blue jeans. "You want to whore yourself out, Madison. Get on your knees and show me what you've still got."

"I hate you."

"Then the door is right there."

Seconds passed; the ticking of the proverbial clock echoed in our heads until Madison made her decision.

Falling to her knees, she kept her eyes on the prize.

Chapter 25

Julia
Present day

*M*ichael opened the cabin door and stepped inside before opening it wide and welcoming us within. Paula was the first to enter, followed by Margaret, and then me.

Paula shook her head as she took in the old cabin. "This place hasn't changed." Warm vapors hung in the frigid interior air.

"You've been here before?" I asked.

A smile came to her lips. "Long ago, this was a place where people would get away."

"Away?"

"You know," Margaret replied, "kind of like parking without the car."

My mouth gaped open as I stared at the older woman. "With your husband?"

Paula laughed. "He wasn't my husband then."

"Don't encourage her," Margaret said. "I'm due years of therapy. This conversation will just add extra sessions."

I couldn't help but giggle at the relationship Paula and Margaret had. They were carefree and fun while being able to work well together. As I watched and listened, I made a mental goal of one day being that kind of mother. One day I could make a daughter uncomfortable talking about how her mother and father met while maintaining a healthy relationship—something my mother and I had missed.

Was I really thinking about having children with Van?

Paula's reminiscing spurred a question. "How long has the cabin been here?"

"Before me," Paula replied. "Some say over two hundred years."

Standing in the middle of the room, I spun around, taking in all its sights with the benefit of daylight shining through the old windows. The aged glass was foggy and bubbled. I walked to the window in the kitchen area and rubbed the pane with my glove. Some of the smudge stirred, yet the lack of transparency made me question what I thought I'd seen. "Do you think I'm crazy for wanting to marry out here?"

Margaret smiled. "Some might say you're crazy for wanting to marry Donovan."

"Peggy," Paula reprimanded.

My smile grew. "And those people might be right. I'm sure with my new runaway bride title, some think the same of him."

"I would bet Mr. Sherman," Paula said, "would marry you anywhere you choose."

I remembered what he'd said last night. "He mentioned a fishing hut out on the bay." I rubbed my gloved hands together. "It would probably be equally as warm."

"Since electricity is out of the question," Margaret said, "tell us what you were thinking."

"I mean, I really hadn't..."

"You told me that your wedding was in your mind," she said, encouraging me. "Tell me and Mom what you see in those thoughts."

I took a deep breath and closed my eyes. In only a few visits, I could picture the entirety of the cabin's interior. From the handmade furniture to the old water pump in the kitchen sink. I recalled the blankets layered on the bed and the waders hanging in the skinny cabinet.

Opening my eyes, I gestured toward the fireplace. "I imagined we'd say our vows over here." I turned. "We could move the furniture so our honored guests" —I grinned— "*you* have a place to sit. And then after our vows, we could celebrate with something simple around the small table. Maybe wine and cake."

"Do you have a theme?" Margaret asked.

"No. My mother did all the planning for my first wedding." I shrugged. "Second, too."

"Those don't count," she said. "This is your real wedding."

I continued to peer up at the rafters and around at the wood walls. "My mother would not approve."

Paula's gloved hand covered mine. "Lace, bows, flowers. Tell us about your dress."

I scoffed. "I don't have one."

"If I didn't know better, I'd wonder if you realized who you were marrying. He'd spare no expense."

"I guess after the first debacle of a wedding, I realized that it isn't the production that matters. It's the person I'm marrying. And I do know who he is—as much as I've learned so far. I have the feeling there's a lot left to learn." I took a breath. "I know he'd spend whatever I asked. My parents might even chip in... again. And I'm not without my own funds. I don't want any of that." I walked back to the fireplace. "I want Van and me here, where we first got to know one another, in front of a roaring fire, proclaiming our forever."

I gripped the wood frame of the sofa. "Do you think Van made the furniture?"

Paula was the one to answer. "The furniture has been here. Mr. Sherman had new cushions made, but the furniture is presumably as old as the cabin, made from local wood. Some believe that the builder was a trapper. He would come up to these parts from the south in the summer and trap for fur. Fox. Beaver. Wolf. Bear."

"Bear?"

Both ladies smiled. "Not as many of those around."

A shiver ran through me, remembering the sight beyond the window. "Could a bear see into the cabin?"

Paula nodded. "That's why Mr. Sherman is careful about leaving perishable food out here."

"What happened to the man?" I asked.

"No one knows for sure. No one even knows if the legend is real. Back then the land was free to roam and squat. No deeds. No records. Truth is, it might not have been someone from the south of what would become Wisconsin. It could have been a member of a local tribe. No one much cared about this territory until they discovered its hidden treasure."

I was fascinated. "What treasure?"

"Lead. The fur trade was superseded by mining. The builder of the cabin may have died south where most would spend their winters, or he could have been a casualty of the many wars and territorial disputes in this area. By the time Wisconsin became a state, most of the original inhabitants were forced from their lands and pushed west or confined to reservations."

My nose scrunched. "That's sad."

"It is," Paula agreed.

I thought about my fiancé. "Van's desire to own more isn't new."

Paula shook her head. "As old as time. The process has become more refined and accepted, but it's still the same. This cabin is a memory of a time long ago. It shows those who enter it a time when life was much harder than it is today."

"Harder?" I questioned. "It represents simplicity to me."

"Imagine living here all summer."

I scoffed, thinking about the lack of fresh water, electricity, or even cell phone service. "Okay, you win. That would be hard."

"Your water came from the lake, nearly a quarter mile away," Margaret said. "You chopped wood for heat and for fuel to cook."

I lifted my hands. "I get it. Furniture was made, not bought."

"Many forms of currency were worthless to the natives. Commodities were bartered and traded." Paula grinned. "Mr. Sherman once told my husband that he wanted to keep the cabin as a monument to those who had loved this land before life became complicated. Bruce told him the truth."

"What is that?" I asked.

"Life is always complicated. What appears simple for one is difficult for others. The trick is to embrace the complication."

Letting out a breath, I nodded. "That's what I'm determined to do."

"Like I said," Paula went on, "complicated men need love too. And so do complicated women."

I slowly spun around, looking anew at the one room. "I would love simple decorations. Whatever you think would be best. I trust you. And we don't need a lot of food. Just enough to celebrate."

"We can do that," Margaret said. "Now, what about your dress?"

"Didn't you say there were some boutiques in town?"

"I did. Do you want help?"

"I've asked too much of you."

"You haven't," she said, "but I won't intrude."

"I think I want to pick out the dress myself."

Both women nodded.

"I can't thank you enough for your help."

"Leave the cabin and celebration to us," Margaret said. "You get your dress and concentrate on the most important part of a wedding, the bride and groom."

The next morning, after breakfast, Albert drove me into Ashland. Convincing him to watch me from afar, I walked along the sidewalk on my way to a boutique I found online, one I hoped would have a dress. I was looking in store windows when my new phone rang. Stepping inside a coffee shop to get out of the cold, I checked the number.

Hurriedly, I answered. "Vicki."

"I'm sorry it's been so hard for me to return your call," she said. "I can't tell you how relieved I was to hear from you. Last week was bizarre."

"That's one word for it," I said, lowering my voice as I peered around the almost-empty shop brimming with the magical aroma of coffee beans in all flavors.

After ordering a chocolate latte, I settled into a back booth, shaking off my coat, hat, and gloves. "You got my long text about Phillip?"

"I did. It's crazy."

"It is, but I'm not going to let it stop us. We're really going to do it."

"There are so many options on what you might do with that sexy man."

"Get married," I said with a grin.

"The two of you?"

I nodded, though she couldn't see me. "Yes. Van and I applied for our license. We're going to marry on Saturday."

"Gah, Jules. I want to be there."

"Ashland is only a seven-hour drive. Or we could send a plane." I didn't want to assume, but Van had said whatever I wanted.

"Who's standing up with you?"

"No one...unless you're here."

"What about your parents?" she asked.

I took a sip of the warm chocolate brew. "My mom forfeited any rights she had at that farce last week."

"In her defense," Vicki said, "she thought Phillip was Van."

"Even so, she did what she always has done. She didn't or wouldn't listen to me. I told her I didn't want to marry and what did she do? She invited one hundred people."

"I get it," she said. "I don't know if Ana is capable of not going overboard."

"That's it in a nutshell. I don't want overboard with Van." I thought about what Paula had said. "Mom would find it impossible to let me have the wedding I want."

"And what is that?"

"I told you about the cabin. That's what I want. It's simple. It's without an aesthetician or expensive dress or any of the hoopla."

"You know," Vicki said, "when I was looking up stuff about Van, I saw where he was named most eligible bachelor."

"That was a decade ago."

"So now he's more eligible, right?"

"No." I smiled. "Now, he's taken."

Vicki laughed. "It's funny that a man who can afford the moon and stars and one who other women have pined over is going to get married in a backwoods cabin without electricity."

"I don't think he minds."

"I think it's cool."

"So can you be here?"

"I'll try, Jules. Text me all the information, and I'll get back to you."

I tugged on my lip. "I really want you here."

"I'm oh for two," she said with a giggle. "I don't want to miss the real one."

"We have room for you to stay. Either tell me you need transportation or you get to Van's house. I'll send you his address." I remembered the new gate. "Oh, there's a gate. Let me know when you're coming, and I'll alert security."

"Fancy."

"No," I replied, "a pain. But it makes Van happy, and

if I were to be completely honest, I'm still freaked out about Phillip."

"Yeah, I talked to him—when I thought he was Van —I agree he was off. It just seemed odd. I had no clue he wasn't Van and neither did your mom."

"I appreciate you sticking up for her, but not knowing Phillip from Van wasn't as upsetting as things she did and said." I thought about the conversation. "She said I'd prostituted myself for Wade."

"She what?" Vicki gasped.

I looked around, lowering my voice. "I'm done letting her run my life."

"Does she know about Saturday?"

"No," I said, taking another chocolaty sip. "I'll inform her and Dad after it's done."

"I'll do my best to be there."

"That's all I can ask."

After the call and my coffee was done, I put back on my coat, hat, and gloves and waved goodbye to the barista. She had a new customer at the counter. As I began to walk away, I turned back.

The two women were talking.

I couldn't place what it was about the woman, but the customer seemed familiar.

Soon my thoughts were filled with Vicki's promise to attend the wedding and my search for a perfect new dress.

Julia

Thursday afternoon I was in the library refreshing my memory on my research of Wade. I'd told Van I would wait until I could claim my shares, but I needed to stay busy. It seemed that our stay in Chicago had created some backlog for Van at his office. Since Monday morning he was off early and home after the sun set.

Wandering around the big house even with the new security had my nerves stretched taut. While I assumed it was the new security system, I couldn't shake the sense that I was being watched. I'd even check the app to see myself as a heat bubble on the floor plan. Earlier in the morning, I'd gone up to the third floor. While I'd entered the large room with the paintings weeks ago, now the door was locked.

I ran my fingers over the doorframe searching for a key and found none.

The heat sensors for the space were on backorder; that was what Jonathon had said when he programmed my handprint into the outer-door sensors. I told myself that was why the room was locked, just like the other unused rooms on the second floor.

Everything about our wedding I'd delegated to Paula and Margaret. Too much spare time allowed me to think about things I wanted to forget or encouraged my overactive imagination. Submerging myself in the profit-and-loss reports from the first three quarters of last year as well as the estimated expenditures for this year was keeping my mind occupied.

Sometime after lunch, I startled when the new alarm system signaled the opening of the kitchen door from the garage. A quick look at my new app showed me that the alarms had been disabled. That meant either a member of the security or my wedding planners were coming into the house or possibly that Van was home.

Judging by the time of day, I was most certain it was either security or Margaret and Paula with questions about the wedding. I stood, pushing away from the table and screens as thoughts of decorating samples or ideas came to mind.

The maze of hallways that only weeks ago seemed complex, were all familiar passages as I made my way toward the front of the house. Just before reaching the staircase, I saw the man I didn't expect to see. His sexy stare met mine as his smile grew.

The millisecond of hesitation went unnoticed. Yet I couldn't stop my concern that my eyes weren't seeing who I thought they were.

"What are you doing home?" I asked, forcing a smile and hurrying toward Van.

As soon as we touched, my apprehension disappeared.

The tingle of electricity that sparked at our connection couldn't be feigned. Our bodies and beings knew one another, even when my mind and sight feared otherwise.

His hands warmed my cheeks. "I feel like I've been working too much the last few days. I'm missing out on spending time with my favorite person."

"And who would that person be?" I lifted my arms to his shoulders as I raised myself to my tiptoes and brushed his lips with mine.

Van's hands moved to my waist, his fingers splaying beneath the camisole under my sweater and pulling me against him. "I think we should do something."

"What kind of something?" I asked suggestively.

"Okay, now you're changing my mind."

I settled down upon my stocking feet. "What were you thinking?"

"To get you out of the house."

My body tensed before I could stop it. "I went to Ashland on Tuesday, remember."

"I haven't seen proof of that."

"That's because you can't see the dress I found."

"A few weeks ago, we talked about something, and we haven't done it."

I tried to search my memories. "I'm not sure of

anything we haven't done."

Van shook his head. "Listen to you. I'm trying to get you out in the fresh air, and you keep taking the subject back to sex."

My eyes opened wide. "What can we do outside? It's freezing."

"I'll have you know, it's a balmy twenty-eight degrees Fahrenheit. That's practically bathing suit weather around here."

"Yeah, I'm not swimming. Or is there a hot spring?"

"No, beautiful. No swimming. I told you about snowmobiling. The ice on the bay is now safe enough for cars. I was watching the locals from my window at work and when my afternoon appointment rescheduled, I decided to surprise you."

I peered from Van's expression to the large windows. Despite my uneasiness with leaving the house, the gleam in his green eyes was enough for me to agree to his idea. "Snowmobile?"

Van nodded.

"On the bay?"

"On our land and the bay. I'll show you around more."

"What about our security?"

"I already filled them in on our plans."

"I hadn't agreed," I said with a grin.

"I was planning on persuading you." Van kissed my nose. "Negotiation is my specialty."

"Getting your way is your specialty."

"There is that," he said with a grin.

The more the idea settled in, the more excited I became. "Does this mean to dress in layers?"

"Yes, and then cover it all with a snowmobile suit. It's like ski-wear but one big jumpsuit."

"Yeah, I don't have one of those," I said.

"You do now. It's in the kitchen."

I shook my head. "How is it that every time I use attire as an excuse, you have that covered?"

"Because, Julia, I'm getting to know how your mind works, and I'm a step ahead."

I narrowed my gaze. "What am I thinking now?"

Van's lips quirked. "I know what I'm thinking." He tugged my hand, pulling me toward the kitchen. When we stopped, the jumpsuit he'd described was lying on the kitchen table.

"It's big."

"It's warm." His lips came to my neck. "But don't worry. I have plans to help you shed it later today."

"Well," I said, picking up the shiny material. "At least I know I won't be stuck in it all night."

"You definitely won't be."

I felt like the abominable snowman as we entered the bay of garages. Van handed me a helmet. "Instead of my hat?"

"No, over your hat. And put your sunglasses beneath the visor."

He pulled the snowmobile out of one of the garages and onto the snow-packed lane beyond the driveway. As

he revved the engine, my thoughts went to the moun-
tain man who saved me. This man with the layers of
outerwear, sunglasses, helmet, and boots wasn't the
Donovan Sherman others knew or could even research.
This was the man I loved, wanting to share something
new with me.

Our helmets had microphones allowing us to
converse.

"Get on the back like you would a motorcycle and
hold on tight to me," Van said.

As I complied, I said, "This is my first time riding a
snowmobile."

Van's smile flashed over his shoulder as he craned his
neck toward me. "You know how I feel about firsts."

I wrapped my arms around his torso and leaned my
body against his when all at once, he hit the accelerator
and we took off. I gasped at the speed and the wind
against our bodies. Van's deep laugh calmed me as he
weaved us around trees until we came to a wide clearing
—a path between trees.

"When the snow is gone," he said, "this is a lane of
sorts. We have four wheelers to drive through here. A
truck would make it, but I prefer to keep the large
motorized vehicles to a minimum."

"Where are we going?"

"I want to show you what it's like to ride on water."

"Water?"

"Frozen water. The surface is solid, smooth, and
wide open. It's exhilarating."

My cheeks tingled yet the outerwear was doing its job, keeping me warm as Van whisked us over his property and out onto the vast expanse of Chequamegon Bay. Loose snow scattered behind us much like a long white tail as we glided over the surface.

As the sky above us filled with pink and red hues, our speed decreased, and we headed back toward the shore.

"Do you know where we are?" I asked, hopeful we weren't lost. Nothing stood out as unique in the picturesque winter scene.

"I do. I've spent a lot of time out here."

"Are we headed home?"

"I have one more stop."

Nestling close to Van, the roar of the engine soothed me as we made our way on paths between tall trees that I hoped he knew how to navigate. The sun was almost set when we came upon a familiar setting.

"The cabin?" I squinted through the sunglasses and visor as my pulse increased. "There's light inside."

"There is," Van replied.

Soon he had the snowmobile nearly to the small cabin. As he did, an SUV I recognized as Michael's new vehicle came into view. My pulse returned to normal at the relief of the familiar vehicle. "Michael is here."

"He is now."

My arms and legs tingled as Van cut the engine and I lifted myself from the wide seat. "I think I might need a massage."

After tugging his mittens from his hands, Van removed my helmet and sunglasses. "You won't need these."

We stomped the snow from our boots as we neared the cabin.

When Van opened the door, we were met by a gust of warm air filled with the scent of burning pine. A smile lifted my cool cheeks as I took in the fireplace, the woodbin filled with cut logs, and the kitchen table, covered with a tablecloth.

"You did all this?"

"I had help." His gaze went toward Michael who smiled, nodded, and bid us goodnight.

"Good night?" I looked around. "You want to spend the night out here?"

Van's palms came to my cheeks. "This is our place, Julia. No one can change that. In two days, we're going to marry right here in front of the fire. This is where we first made love, where I asked you to marry me, a real proposal. This is our space. Saturday, I want you to feel as comfortable here as you did that very first night."

I blinked away the tears.

For the first time since Phillip tried to tear us apart and someone violated our space, my tears were happy. "You did this for me? You had it planned since we got on the snowmobile?"

Van pulled the hat from his head, leaving his dark mane a mess and grinned. Despite the visor, his cheeks were pink from the cold and wind. "I had it planned before that. The snowmobile suit didn't arrive until today."

I too pulled my mittens from my hands and the hat from my head. "You know, I'm as much of a mess as I was that first night." I turned to the door. "You will lock that?"

"I'll lock it." He tilted his head to the kitchen counter. "It's a bit old-fashioned, but now we have a battery-operated CB. Our phones won't work, but we can radio Michael or Albert if we need anything."

Shaking my head, I wrapped my arms around Van's torso. "I love you more every day."

"You know me, more is better." His expression turned serious. "We can leave and go back to the house if you want."

"I don't want that."

Breaking away, he pointed to the table. "We even have Mrs. Mayhand's cooking. It's staying warm in the oven."

"Is there anything you didn't think of?" I asked.

He took a step toward me and reached for the zipper on the front of the snowsuit. "I believe the next order of business on our agenda is one of my favorite activities." He pulled the long zipper until it was near my thigh. "Undressing you."

I did the same, pulling the zipper on the front of his jumpsuit. "Only if you get to join me in my undressed state."

Chapter 27

Van

Less than eleven years ago

"Come with me," I said. It was as if my voice weren't audible. Perhaps it was only in my own head. "Madison."

She turned my way, her green eyes glassy as if the world was no longer in focus.

I went closer. "Let's get out of the house."

"He's coming."

Her words were a direct hit, a kill shot to what was left of my heart. The one sentence hurt more than I wanted to admit, but it wasn't a surprise. No, I'd been expecting it since the day Madison got the test result she'd wanted.

He was coming.

Phillip was on his way to take his wife and the baby within her.

Walking away, I gathered my thoughts as I entered the neighboring bedroom and flipped the light switch. The artificial illumination wasn't necessary—the autumn sunshine through the corner windows filled the room. It was why she'd chosen this room.

Madison's latest painting was still on the easel. Last night when I'd gone to bed, the work was incomplete. As I stared, I saw that she'd finished.

"It's beautiful and sad."

I turned, finding her standing in the doorway, a waif or maybe a ghost. It was what her presence had become. Only a few weeks pregnant, Madison's first sign was nausea. It didn't only hit in the morning. The sickness had taken its toll, lowering her weight, energy, and enthusiasm. Her cheekbones had become more prominent. Her watch hung from her thinning wrist. The walks she took around the property while I worked did little to bring color to her pale skin.

Madison was fading away.

It would happen whether I kept her here or if she left.

I felt that reality deep within me.

"They say she was paralyzed," Madison said, looking at the painting. "A degenerative disease."

I'd seen the artwork in one of the many books I'd brought to the house. It was entitled *Christina's World*. Madison had even replicated the artist's signature. The book was open and lying on the nearby table. Her dedication to detail was impressive. If I didn't know better, I'd believe we were looking at the original work.

"I don't think she is," Madison continued, tilting her

head and staring at the figure of the girl upon the grass. "I think she's stuck."

The girl in the painting appeared to be looking at a house at the top of an open field.

"You see," Madison went on, "she's caught between the stark reality that winter is coming and what she must give up. The colors the original artist used were to represent the autumn season. New growth is gone. The grass is brown and dying. New birth is a way in the distance."

"Doesn't she want winter?"

"No. She wants life. Springtime is life. Winter is cold and bleak." She turned to the windows. Beyond the panes, many of the deciduous trees were sporting their colors. Reds, yellows, and oranges abounded where only weeks earlier there had been green. "I couldn't do winter here, Van. I wouldn't make it."

There was no convincing Madison to stay. I knew that.

In the middle of the night, I'd wake with the nightmare that my dream had come true, that she was beside me. Our child was in the room down the hall. I'd wake in a sweat with my heart pounding.

The vision in my dream was what my mind thought it wanted. My body's reaction was the reality of what that would mean. Keeping Madison would be a constant battle, a chore that never ended. Despite Lena's warnings, I'd been blind to her frailty.

Sometimes it was difficult to fathom that Madison

and Lena were sisters and had been born of the same parents. Where Lena had strength, Madison had a void in constant need of filling. It was tiresome and wearing.

Sharing genetics was no guarantee of commonality. I knew that personally.

One day Madison's art would make her happy. She'd paint and flit around the studio room like a bright bird filled with promise, hopping from branch to branch. Her smile would take away even the dark clouds before a rainstorm. And then for two or three days, she'd barely move.

Getting her to get out of bed or bathe was a chore.

I'd talked to her and to Lena about doctors.

I'd read about conditions that were no fault of Madison's. Medications and therapy could help. I'd almost had her convinced to seek treatment when the pregnancy test came back positive.

Madison dug in her heels.

She claimed she didn't need treatment. She needed a child.

Madison had accomplished the goal she set when she showed up at my doorstep. In her mind, once she was back to her life with her husband and child, she would be better.

It was during her non-better times that I saw the battle she fought. Her accusations during those lows were no longer as hurtful as the emptiness in her gaze.

In her mind, I was the cause of her woes.

I'd held her prisoner here against her will.

Of course, the door was never locked. The telephone and computer were at her disposal.

As each day passed and her life's shine diminished, I saw myself for the man she saw. I was the monster who made her step away from her life. And now I was the reason she wouldn't seek professional help.

I was the monster she claimed me to be.

"The new house is done," I said. "Come see it with me."

"I...I." She looked around the art studio we'd created. "I can't take this with me."

"No room in your little house?" I never said I wasn't cruel. "Or won't Phillip understand?"

She wrapped her arms around her stomach. "Both. He thinks painting is frivolous and we'll need the space for the baby."

I offered her my hand. "Come with me. It won't take long. I want you to be fully aware of what you're leaving."

"I'm not leaving, Van." Her volume rose. "I'm going back to my life. My life. Don't you understand? This isn't my life. I don't want this." She reached for paintings leaning against the wall and shoved them until they fell like dominos, one hitting the other." Once they were down, her expression changed, as if she suddenly realized what she'd done.

Her panic was real.

"Madison, it's all right."

"No. No. I'm sorry." Her hands shook as she tried to right each canvas.

I reached for her shoulder. "Stop. The paintings are fine."

She pulled herself back as if my touch was covered with acid, burning her skin as her eyes opened wide. "I'm sorry, Phillip. I didn't mean..."

I took a deep breath.

Anger wouldn't help. It was only when she believed I was upset that she called me by my brother's name. Steadying my voice, I spoke slowly. "Come on, Madison. I have something to show you."

I wasn't sure when Phillip would arrive. The new house was over a mile away. With the autumn temperature and sunshine, I'd gladly walk, but I didn't want to worry her about not being back for her rescue.

Taking my truck, we drove down one lane, back to the main road and to the new driveway leading to the house I'd imagined. Madison's focus stayed beyond the truck's windows as the tires bumped over uneven roadway. It was as the new home came into view that she seemed to recognize that we'd found a new destination.

"Oh, Van, this is stunning."

It was.

I'd chosen the best house with the best view. Bruce Mayhand was my contractor. The renovation took months and months, bordering on a year. The final product was worth every minute and penny, especially if I could convince Madison to stay.

With her hand in mine, we stepped up the front stairs. Her lips opened as she stared up at the grand front door.

"Everything is so big."

"Bigger and better," I said.

Opening the inner French doors, Madison stopped at the threshold. The interior was finished and cavernous without furnishings. "Those windows."

"I love seeing the bay," I said. It was more than the blue waters. The land around the bay was a colorful explosion of leaves. It was almost as if the forest was ablaze.

Taking her hand, I led her up the stairs and up to the third floor.

The door opened to a large expanse. Originally, I'd wanted my office up here. The view beyond the windows was remarkable. But in the last two and a half months, I'd given Bruce a new directive. This was to be an art studio.

Madison slowly spun, taking in the space and the light.

"This room is for you."

"Oh, it's big enough for my painting and a nursery." Her expression of wonder quickly faded. "No. I don't want this."

Swallowing, I nodded. "I know. It's still here."

"I belong with Phillip."

She didn't.

That wasn't a battle I would win.

"Then let's go back. He should be here soon."

Once we were on the first floor, I took her to the breezeway between the garage and house. There was one inconspicuous door within the windows leading to the outside. "Let me show you something."

"I won't remember. I don't want to know."

"It doesn't matter. I want you to know."

Beside the door on the outside was a small box. To most it would appear to be an electrical box. Opening the top case, I pulled out a key. "I'll leave this here, Madison. I swear it will never go away."

The autumn breeze blew her hair around her thinning face. "Why?"

"You'll always have a place here."

She shook her head.

"I'm not asking. I'm not going to stop you from leaving. I want you to know that even though the house where our child was conceived will soon be gone, you and our child will always have a home here."

A cascade of tears slithered down her cheeks, yet Madison didn't make a sound. Instead, she lifted her chin toward the sky, closed her eyes, and hummed. "This will be goodbye." She turned to me. "You promised."

"What will he do? What will he say? He'll know the child is mine."

Madison's lips quivered. "I'll make him understand."

I offered her my hand one last time. "Let's go."

If I'd expected any common sense from my brother

upon his arrival, I'd been mistaken. His anger wasn't only directed at me. I couldn't blame him. Once again, I'd accomplished what he never would.

Standing at the railing on the second floor, I watched as they left.

After they drove away, I called Bruce, telling him I would move into the new house immediately. Furniture could wait.

I wasn't spending another night in the house Madison and I'd shared, if only for a few months.

Chapter 28

Van
Present day

*M*y eyes opened and I sat up, the blankets on the bed moving down my body as I caught my breath. I searched the darkness, not sure what I would find. It took only seconds or less for me to realize whatever the fuck had been going on wasn't real.

What the hell were dreams or nightmares composed of?

Repressed memories, forgotten absurdities.

Just because it wasn't real didn't mean my heart wasn't racing or my skin clammy with perspiration.

"Shit."

I laid my hand on Julia's shoulder, splaying my fingers over the warmth of her bare skin. The world was right. She was sleeping beside me, where I wanted her for eternity.

Allowing my pulse to even, I fluffed my pillow and laid my head on my fist, staring through the darkness of our suite at the most beautiful woman I'd ever had the opportunity to love.

She'd asked me a few nights ago what I was like at her age. The real answer was that years ago I was a man who didn't deserve her. Fuck. I didn't deserve Julia now, but I was different.

Falling back onto my pillow, I stared up at the ceiling.

I'd made my share of mistakes.

I'd made more than my share.

Vengeance and disgust were powerful motivators. They bred ruthless success as well as horrible actions. What separated men like me from the ones rotting behind prison bars was simple—money. My crimes weren't what fueled my success as a businessman. My success as a businessman helped to hide my crimes.

Phillip's resurrection with the help of the Butlers threatened my newfound life.

I wanted to continue the battle we'd begun years ago. The desire to see the Butlers and members of my family fall into a hopeless pit was enticing and obtainable. It was within reach. The problem was that every scenario to fuck the Butlers had ripples. Repercussions would eventually reach Julia.

Phillip would pay for what he did.

Tricking and scaring Julia was uncalled for. She was the only innocent one in this interesting mix of people. There were two—her and Brooklyn.

Then again, that conceived in sin...

Fuck Phillip.

Fuck Madison.

Fuck them all.

I'd be sure to follow through with my revenge.

The Butlers would lose, but not as much as they could. If they did, it would bite the McGraths and ultimately, Julia. That hardly meant I was letting them off the hook. It was one fucking battle. In the end, the war was mine. We had many battles to go.

What I didn't need were reminders of the past.

I'd been waiting to hear how Lena's visit with Madison went. The thought of Madison even more out of touch with reality didn't bring me joy.

Was that Julia's influence?

Madison deserved to be Brooklyn's mother even if neither Phillip nor I deserved to be her father. If Lena found the answer Madison needed, I'd offer to help. Lena was probably right that we all had our share of blame.

My thoughts went back to the night Phillip was on my property, when he came for Madison. Closing my eyes tightly, I saw her. I was standing on the second floor, demanding him to leave, to leave her alone.

Their marriage wasn't simply a fairy tale without a happy ending. No, there was a darkness in Madison that hadn't been present before. It came out first in her paintings and later in her confessions.

She was going to walk away with my child to go to a man who was too fucked up to appreciate the gift she'd helped create for him.

My stomach knotted as it did that night.

I said things, threatened things...

With an exhale, I let it go.

I was done.

Julia was my future.

My past was filled with chaos that cleared the path for what would come.

Now I knew what that promise was all about.

That promise was Julia.

She was lying beside me, ready and willing to take the title no one else had taken. Julia was to become my wife. My real wife.

I marveled at the way the sheet hung over Julia's hips to her waist. With her back to me, I had the perfect view of her curves, the crest of her breasts, and the way her hair fanned behind her in a golden veil.

My thoughts slipped back to Thursday night in the cabin.

As the night faded into morning, I watched with relief the change in Julia. She was so responsive and still trusting. It wasn't bad. It was refreshing.

Her willingness to see beyond the ugliness of the world and to believe in us. It was as if she saw a me I'd never known. She brought that person out by simply being herself. With her I'd become a person who craved to be better, to want the more, bigger, and better, but no longer in the manic way I had.

The distractions of the last week faded into background noise as in the cabin we took back what we'd lost. The two of us alone with the fire and each other for heat, we came together. I craved everything about her.

Her laugh.

Her smile.

The tone of her voice.

The noises she made.

The way her body tensed just before she came undone.

It was as we left the cabin on Friday morning that Julia reconfirmed what I knew deep within my once dead soul. She was mine. Julia was made for me, presented to me at a time when I could appreciate the gift she was, could spend time and energy making her every dream a reality, and could finally allow myself of what I'd forever been deprived.

Love.

Michael and Albert picked us up, lifting the snowmobile into the bed of the truck. As we drove toward the lane, Julia reached for my hand.

"I don't know how you do it," she said.

"I don't know what it is, but if you like it, I'll try to keep doing it."

"You hear me even when I don't talk."

In all fairness, I wasn't exactly sure what she meant until we were back at the house.

"How did you know I was apprehensive about the cabin?" she asked.

The truthful answer was that I knew because I shared her concern. Instead, I asked, "Are you still?"

"No. Just like everything else that's felt broken in our snow globe, you fixed it."

Now, on the morning of our wedding, I couldn't stop thinking about what it would mean to marry Julia. I'd never wanted something so unobtainable this much in my life. What we shared was unexplainable in a way that didn't need to be explained.

All of the mistakes and terrible things I'd done in my life couldn't be forgotten. They were as much a part of me as my striving for the next trophy. However, with Julia, I was more concerned about moving forward than looking back.

I ran my fingertips over her shoulder, arm, hips...

"Van..." My name came out sleepily with the melody of her laugh.

Julia rolled onto her back, her blue eyes blinking as she focused through the darkness. "What time is it?"

"It's our wedding day."

Chapter 29

Van

Her petite hands came up, her arms encircling my neck as I stared down at her. "I promise I won't run."

I couldn't help but scoff. "Well, you do have a reputation."

"No, Van. I know what I want. I want you. I want to marry you. All the other times were wrong."

I lowered my forehead to hers. "I don't know how or why the universe dropped you on the road for me to find. I just know I'll never let you go."

Julia wiggled beneath the covers, bringing her hips, core, and warm, sexy body closer.

Smoothing her hair away from her face, I kissed her lips as I found my place between her legs. Without provocation, I was rock hard. My cock teased her swollen entrance.

"Wait," Julia said, her hands coming to my chest. "Isn't this bad luck?"

"Sliding my cock into your wet pussy is the opposite of bad luck."

"But it's our wedding day. You aren't supposed to see me."

"Beautiful, I see you and I want you. I could fuck you twenty times before the ceremony and I promise as soon as we say 'I do,' I'll be ready to fuck you again."

Her giggle rang through the bedroom. "I don't know. You are old."

In one swoop, I rolled, pulling Julia over me as I lay on my back. Her hands landed on my shoulders, her knees fell to both sides of mine, and her hair hung down, creating a curtain around us. "Why did you do that?"

"If I'm so old, I'll let you do the hard work."

"Hmm." Her breasts heaved as she wiggled, situating herself, ready to take me deep inside.

"That's it. Let me watch you."

Julia's eyes closed as she impaled herself, her back arching and lips opening as she lowered her knees. "I love how full I feel."

My hands went to her hips. "Feels fucking fantastic."

I watched with awe as she moved up and down, creating her own rhythm. As I followed her every move, it was as if I could hear a song, a tune providing the melody in the way she moved. It was magical and surreal. All the synonyms that meant fantastic could be shouted from the rooftops as our primitive dance continued.

As Julia's body began to tense, I moved us, rolling until I was staring down into her blue abyss. "I want to wake like this every morning for the rest of my life."

Julia leaned up, her lips brushing mine. "Don't make promises you can't keep."

"Oh, I promise to make you mine every damn day until you're tired of me."

She shook her head. "I won't get tired of you, Van."

Slowly, we continued, kissing and talking, my cock never stopping its pursuit as I thrust in and out. I ran my hands over her, caressing and sculpting. My lips and teeth teased, marking her skin in places only I'd see, until there was no holding her back.

Julia clung to my neck as she detonated around me.

Fucking fireworks on the Fourth of July had nothing on Julia. The New Year's celebration in Sydney Harbour paled. She was a celebration to be near, a gift to love, and more than I ever imagined.

When Julia lifted her chin and smiled, I asked, "Will you marry me?"

"Only today and only for forever."

It was hardly the moment, but I had just finalized the paperwork last night and time was running out. This was something Oscar Fields had wanted since I first floated the idea of marrying Julia. However, the final document wasn't exactly as he'd recommended.

I smoothed her long hair over her shoulders. "It isn't much of a wedding gift, but I have something downstairs for you to sign."

Julia's gaze narrowed. "Sign?"

"It's a prenuptial agreement."

"I didn't think we were doing that."

"You don't have to sign it, Julia. But I promise it's for you, not me."

Our union ended as she scooted up to the headboard and pulled the sheet over her breasts. "I don't want your money, Van."

I took a deep breath. "I don't want to talk about this today."

"Well, if I'm supposed to sign, I think it's our last chance."

Pushing the sheets away I stood, fully nude and still semi-erect. Running my hand over my hair, I said what I should have said after my conversation with Ashley from GreenSphere and especially after what my team learned about the complaint against her grandfather's will. "I want you to believe that I want Wade to succeed."

Her jaw set. "I feel like there is going to be a *but*..."

"It wasn't a sure investment. You knew that."

"Van, why are we discussing this now?"

"Because today after we marry, you will have the official rights to your family's shares."

"And this couldn't wait?"

"I'll go into as much or as little detail as you want, but the important part is that your family's shares are in jeopardy if the complaint against your grandfather's will goes forward. There's evidence, or the law firm is claiming that they have evidence, that the will was doctored after your grandfather's death."

Julia pulled the sheet higher. "No. That's not right. My parents wouldn't—"

I knelt onto the bed beside her. "Nothing is proven. My legal team hasn't been able to learn more than what they could find in filings. If your shares became mine, I could possibly stop the court from seizing them through the investigation."

"Is that what's in the prenup?"

I shook my head. "No. It's what Oscar Fields and a slew of other legal minds told me to put in the prenup."

"What is in it?"

I reached for her hand. "Julia, when I found you, I had no idea who you were. Our first night in the cabin was the most open and honest I'd been in" —I took a breath— "possibly my entire life. I've told you that I've done bad things. But that all changed in one night and I can't un-change that even if I wanted to. Once I got back to the office and I saw your name on my schedule, I kicked into the mode I'd done for the last twenty-plus years, sizing, evaluating, looking for weakness, and seizing opportunity. I saw you as a chance to rekindle a fight, one I had left unfinished. I realized who you were and soon saw an opening to fuck with the Butlers."

"You used me?"

"No, Julia. I love you. I can't say that enough or loud enough. Your family's shares are in jeopardy. That isn't some kind of hyperbole. It's a fact. I was offered a great deal of money and an opportunity for investment to sell my shares and yours. Wade would eventually cease to exist. I'm laying it on the line."

Julia pushed against me, pulling the sheet from the bed and wrapping it around her sexy frame as she stood. "You lied."

"Fuck no." I inhaled. "Let me show you the agreement."

She shook her head. "I was so stupid."

"Julia, the agreement forbids me from selling your stocks."

"What?" She turned my way. "I don't understand."

"It's a loophole, one my lawyers believe will save your family's stocks. The company that made me the offer has already made that same offer to the Butlers and your parents among other investors. Your parents couldn't take the deal because of the decree you handed your mother. They would need your approval."

"If I'd gone through with that wedding..."

"We can't look back. This is forward. The prenuptial agreement states that the stocks of Wade Pharmaceutical remain in your name upon our marriage until which time *you* decide to sell."

"You think I should sell?"

"It also says," I said, "that you are entitled to all that is mine. As of our vows today, everything I have is also yours."

She shook her head. "I don't want your money."

"This isn't about that."

"Then what is it about?" she asked.

"Wade."

"How can we protect the stock?"

"That's up to you and you alone. One possible out is if you decide to sell them to me."

"Sell them? If I have half of what's yours..."

"It's a one-way street, Julia. The stocks will be yours and yours alone. I don't care what thoughts went through my head as I accumulated the wayward stock shares of Wade. My whole life has changed because of you. I'll do whatever I can to help Wade succeed. If your family loses everything else, I don't care. We can help them if you want, or they can flounder. If you sell me the shares of Wade stock, then they will fall under *our* portfolio thus, my legal team believes, making them immune from the court, and they will also be..."

"Half-mine."

I nodded, walking closer to her and reaching for her shoulders. "It was the best solution we could find."

Julia's gaze met mine. "I don't understand what you get out of this prenuptial agreement. Without one, wouldn't the stocks be ours?"

"Yes, but the sale from you to me makes them untouchable. The court can only seize the value I paid."

"What are you going to pay?" she asked.

Walking to the bedside stand, I found my loose change and walked back, handing Julia a quarter. "Let the court take it."

"Won't that affect the true value?"

"Not if the lawyers work their magic."

"Still, what do you get?"

I reached for her hands and pulled her knuckles to my lips. "You."

Chapter 30

Julia

After our shower, I followed Van down to his office. The document he handed me was multiple pages long.

"I'll get you some coffee while you read," he said.

"I really don't want to spend my wedding morning reading a prenuptial agreement."

"You could have the Wade legal team look it over, but they don't have much time."

Before I could respond, Van looked down at his phone, reading a text. Instead of his frown, a smile spread across his face.

"Good news?"

"If I could give you anything for our wedding," he asked, "what would it be?"

"Not this," I said, setting the papers on his desk.

"You don't have to sign it."

"What happens then?"

"Our property becomes joint, all of it. We take our chances with the pending case involving your grandfather's will and we do our damnedest to make Wade succeed."

"If the court decides there was something illegal with Grandfather's will?"

"They could seize whatever assets are still in your family's name. They could even look to collect losses over the last ten years, sending your parents into arrears."

Reaching for a pen, I turned to the last page and scribbled my name on the line. "There. It's done. It's the last time I'll sign that name."

Van's grin blossomed. "Mrs. Sherman."

"I like it. It has a ring to it."

"Now, that present is waiting."

I settled into one of the chairs across from his desk. "How about coffee and the present can wait?"

He tilted his head, looking all clean-shaven and sexy with gym shorts and a t-shirt. "Okay, but your present will probably get cold."

"What?" I jumped from the chair, wearing my robe and slippers. "What present would get cold?"

"The one waiting outside with Albert."

"A person?" I asked apprehensively.

Van nodded.

Running past him, I hurried to the front door. Opening the French doors, I rushed to the heavy large one. Cold air met me as I flung it open to the sight of my best friend getting out of Albert's SUV.

"Vicki!" I screamed as I ran in place. "You made it."

In no time at all, she was wrapped in my embrace.

"Oh my God. I thought you couldn't make it. I thought you had something for school."

Vicki's eyes were wide as I pulled her into the house. "Nice digs."

"Do people say that anymore?"

"You know, retro is coming back."

I turned in time to see Van leaning against the archway beyond the staircase. His arms were crossed over his wide chest, cheeks raised, and he had a sexy grin.

"When did you know she'd make it?"

Lowering his arms, he came our way. "I knew for sure last night."

"Yeah, we had some arranging to do," Vicki said. "By the way, I like this guy better than the last one you were going to marry."

I couldn't stop my grin. "Me too." I playfully hit her arm. "We aren't talking about him anymore."

"It's great to have you here, Vicki," Van said, offering her his hand. "We were just about to have some coffee. Would you like a cup?"

"Yes," she said too loud. "All the caffeine. Send it my way."

Soon the three of us were sitting in the kitchen, drinking coffee, and eating muffins from Van's favorite bakery in Bayfield. The conversation was light and fun, the way it should be with an old friend.

"So this is kind of in the sticks," she said, looking out the window.

I followed her gaze to the white wonderland. "I hear it's even prettier in the summer."

Vicki picked up her mug and carried it to the large windows beyond the fireplace. "I'll need to come back after the thaw."

"You're always welcome," Van said. He looked down at his watch. "Well, I believe Margaret is to be here soon and that's my cue to get scarce."

Getting down from the tall stool, I went to Van, wrapping my arms around his neck. "For the record, I've never been so sure about a wedding."

His forehead tipped to mine. "Me either."

"You two..." Vicki said, "it's almost disgusting how cute you are."

Van laughed. "It's been a minute since I was called cute."

"Oh, well, it's not just you. It's the two of you," Vicki corrected. "Alone you're just..." Her smile met mine. "Super sexy."

Van's eyebrows danced up and down. "Okay. Girl talk." He leaned down, claiming my lips as my hand came to his smooth cheek.

"I'll see you at the cabin."

"You will."

Vicki and I waited as Van walked away. Once he was gone, her voice was lower but with no less enthusiasm. "Damn, girl. This is the whole package."

I nodded. "And more."

"What does that mean?"

"Nothing. Last week made me realize that Van's past will never be gone, but it also taught me that he'll do whatever he can to keep us protected from it."

Vicki's nose scrunched. "That was his brother at your parents' house. Does he have other family?"

"A sister and parents. Oh, and a niece."

"Are any of them coming?"

I shook my head. "They had a falling-out, or maybe multiple fallings-out." I reached for Vicki's hands and smiled. "Family is who we love, and I love you. I can't believe you're here."

"I wouldn't have made it without Van's help. Now, let me see your wedding dress." She looked around. "You know, sometimes it's nice to keep things small and simple."

"No Ana," I said with a grin.

"That may have been what I was thinking."

I tugged her hand. "Bring your coffee if you want. My dress is upstairs." I stopped. "What are you going to wear during the wedding?"

Vicki shrugged. "I have no idea. Van asked my size."

"He did what?"

"I mean, I said I could wear the bridesmaid dress from weddings one and two. He promised something else."

I caught my lower lip between my teeth. Not only hadn't Van mentioned Vicki's arrival, but he also hadn't said anything about a bridesmaid's dress. "What you're wearing is absolutely perfect."

As we made it to the staircase, the doorbell chimed.

"Are you expecting company?" she asked.

I peeked beyond the French doors. "I'll introduce you to Margaret."

After scanning my handprint, I opened the front door. Margaret came in carrying a garment bag. "Special delivery for a maid of honor."

"Did you all conspire against me?"

"No, Julia," Margaret answered. "We all want this day to be the best it can be. By the way, Mom's at the cabin and the decorations are up. Michael is there keeping an eye on things. Albert is outside, and Jonathon is in charge of bringing the judge."

"Then I guess it's time we go upstairs and get me ready."

Vicki took a step back, scanning me from my slipper-clad feet to my satin robe. "I mean, you look pretty hot already."

"Come upstairs and see my dress."

Chapter 31

Van

A few minutes earlier

As I walked away from Julia and Vicki, I had the oddest sensation.

It was normalcy.

Is that even possible for a man like me?

I slowed my stride and turned back. From this distance, the ladies' words were out of range. Their expressions weren't. The joy on Julia's face, the way her lips gaped as she laughed. It was such a simple gesture and yet somehow it felt monumental.

For a few moments, I watched as the two conversed, mesmerized by the woman about to be my wife. In her robe, with her damp hair tied into a bun on top of her head, and no makeup, Julia was without a doubt the realest and most beautiful woman I'd known.

The old saying about beauty was never truer than with Julia.

Her splendor radiated from within. That wasn't to say she lacked anything from a visual standpoint. It meant that her outward glory was the frosting on the delicacy she was on the inside.

Whether surrounded by the frozen tundra or in a room of people, Julia was a beacon of light. I worried I'd tarnish her, and yet deep down, I believed it was impossible. Her good outweighed my bad. It wasn't up to her to change me, but because of her, I wanted to change.

Julia had no way of knowing what she'd done to me. She could never understand the darkness in the man who found her because from the moment I laid eyes on her, her light began to dissipate the dark.

Her presence, zest for life, and incredible heart restored existence to a barren heart. There were too many things about myself that I hadn't shared. And much as the way she'd reacted to the prenuptial agreement with trust and acceptance, I had another unfamiliar emotion.

It was hope.

Hope that we'd survive.

Hope that our snow globe would never shatter.

Hope that my past sins were paid, and Julia's goodness would carry us through.

As I sat down in my office, I scribbled my name at the bottom of the final page of the agreement, below Julia's. It was no wonder my advisors weren't happy. My determination to make Wade successful at all costs went against common sense.

I should take the offer from GreenSphere, sell all our shares and take a seat on their executive board.

That was their advice.

It wasn't that I didn't understand what was being said or that I sought to lose money. I was bogged down by an unquenchable sense that things weren't as they seemed.

My first question was why would the McGraths alter Herman Wade's last will and testament?

To that end, I had my people digging for previously filed wills. It wasn't uncommon for people to change their wills multiple times prior to their death. A man with the wealth of Herman Wade surely had other older drafts of his will.

How does the current will differ from the previous?

My question wasn't only why Julia's parents would alter the will. It was also curiosity on why the will was being contested now, ten years after Herman Wade's death.

Without the prenuptial agreement, I could sell our Wade shares and wash our hands of the company. It would be the easy and profitable option.

Why?

Why was GreenSphere interested?

Why were they offering me a seat on the executive board?

There were too many questions to walk away.

I couldn't guarantee Wade Pharmaceutical's success. I could promise Julia that I wouldn't turn my back without trying.

I sent Oscar Fields a message letting him know that

both Julia and I had signed the agreement. His happiness wasn't my concern. Julia's was.

Checking my cell phone again, I made a call to Rob Landon. Something wasn't sitting right with me. The first and second call went to his voicemail. Instead of leaving a message, I sent a text asking him to call me soon.

A pop-up on my computer screen told me I had a message from Leonard, the head of cybersecurity at Sherman and Madison. If I didn't have his team working on items regarding Wade, I might decide to wait. After all, our wedding was in a few hours.

The doorbell chimed.

For the first time since upgrading our security, the house was a constant parade of comings and goings.

A quick look at the camera's readout on my computer told me Margaret was here.

A grin lifted my cheeks at the sight of the garment bag in her hand. I'd left the dress color and style up to Margaret. While no one had seen Julia's dress, Margaret at least knew the decorations and what Julia was thinking. All I'd been told was to arrive in a suit. No tuxedo.

Julia wanted simple.

I clicked on the message. The final last will and testament of Herman Wade was filed with the probate court following his passing. Previous copies weren't made public.

The copy that had been filed was identical to the one being contested. I'd read through it before. Again, I skimmed over the scanned pages. Nothing appeared out of place. Nothing jumped out at me.

The executor named was an official at a law firm in Chicago.

Shit, it was Saturday morning, but I gave it a try. A quick search and I had the number of the law firm.

"Cobbs and Wilson," a woman's voice said.

"Hello. I'm looking for a Stephen McCook. Is he still a member of your firm?"

"No, I'm sorry. He's no longer with us. May I be of some assistance?"

"I'm looking into my wife's grandfather's last will and testament. Mr. McCook was the named executor."

"Yes," the woman said, "Mr. McCook handled those duties many years ago."

"Is there anyone I could speak to today who may be knowledgeable regarding Mr. McCook's work?"

"Perhaps if you told me the name of the deceased."

"Herman Wade. It would involve the estate of Herman and Juliette Wade," I replied.

"I'm sorry. I missed your name and your wife's name."

"Donovan Sherman. My wife's maiden name was Julia McGrath." I was a few hours early in proclaiming her as my wife. That didn't stop me.

"Sir, I can only tell you what I told the last person inquiring about this document. Mr. McCook filed Mr. Wade's will with the probate court as required by law."

"Was there anything odd about his filing? Why are you receiving multiple inquiries ten years later?"

"Sir, Mr. McCook is no longer available for consult. We've provided all the requested documents to Abbott and Jones. As I told them, we have no documents prior to the final will."

"Does that mean that your firm only worked with Mr. Wade on his final will and testament?"

"It means we have nothing dating before his final will."

"Could you tell me," I asked, "the date Mr. Wade signed his will?"

"Sir, that is public record."

"You're right. Thank you for your time."

I shook my head as I pulled the PDF up on my screen. On my other screen, I pulled up Herman Wade's obituary.

Herman Wade passed away surrounded by family on April 16...

"Shit," I said to no one. "He signed his will the day before he died."

I sent a message to Leonard asking for him to have his team dig into Herman Wade's records and determine if he had personal legal counsel prior to the firm of Cobbs and Wilson. The answer came back:

Previous documents were underwritten by the legal department at Wade Pharmaceutical. The last filing prior to the will with Cobbs and Wilson was signed by Logan Butler.

As the phone on my desk rang, I replied: *Find out*

who the plaintiff is who hired Abbott and Jones to contest Herman Wade's last will and testament.

"Donovan Sherman," I said in way of answering.

"Mr. Sherman. Michael here."

I sat forward in the chair. "Is everything all right out at the cabin?"

"Yes, sir. I just left for a moment to check my cell signal. I had a couple messages I thought you'd want to hear. The first one was from Mr. Landon. He said you'd told him to reach me if he couldn't reach you."

I lifted my cell phone, wondering why Rob couldn't contact me directly. There were no missed calls. "I did. However, I don't have any missed calls from him. What was his message?"

"He said that Phillip Thomas is in San Antonio with his daughter and your sister."

"Did he give you visual confirmation?"

"No, he simply said to tell you that he appears settled in for a while."

"Settled in?" I repeated. That was odd verbiage. How would Rob know that Phillip was settled?

"Okay. What was the second?"

"The spoon in the sink...the one in the cabin."

"Yes."

"I took the liberty of sending it to my company for analysis."

I sat forward. "Why didn't you tell me?"

"I wasn't sure if it had been washed clean. They came back with one simple conclusion. Identitymatching DNA will take time and their success will depend on whether or not the person's DNA is in a data bank."

"What was the simple conclusion?" I asked.

"It wasn't your brother, Mr. Sherman."

I let out a sigh of relief. "You are sure?"

"Yes. The DNA on the spoon was not male."

"It was a female?"

"Yes, sir. Albert is doing some checking in Ashland and neighboring communities asking about transient people. Not many homeless come this far north with nowhere else to go."

"A female," I said again.

"I thought you'd be happy, sir. It seems Phillip has moved on."

"Thank you for the message. Please head back to the cabin. We don't want any uninvited guests."

"At least we can eliminate one."

Chapter 32

Julia

The three of us entered my old suite. "This is where you will stay," I said to Vicki.

She nodded as she looked around, taking in the view of the bay. Soon we were in the bedroom, and I entered the closet. "I hid the dress from Van."

Vicki and Margaret grinned as I came out carrying the garment bag

"You found this in town?" Margaret asked.

"I did. The woman at the boutique in the old bank building was so nice. She didn't have anything that felt right. She sent me to the secondhand shop on Main Street. Once I saw this dress, I knew it was perfect."

Vicki's eyes widened. "You bought your dress secondhand?"

"I know, scandalous, right?"

"Ana would..." Vicki didn't finish the sentence as we both laughed.

"She wanted me to wear the dress we bought for my wedding to Skylar at Van's and my wedding."

"In all fairness," Vicki said, "I think she was holding out hope that you would still marry Skylar."

I shook my head as I lowered the zipper on the bag.

"Oh," Vicki and Margaret said in unison as I removed the cream lace maxi dress from the bag.

"I swear, it is like it was made for me." I laid it out on the bed. "I know it has spaghetti straps, but wait until you see what else the nice woman from the consignment shop found." I hurried in and out of the closet carrying a second garment bag. "This is even better than the dress." Lowering the zipper, I removed the garment from the bag.

"Oh my God," Vicki gushed as she ran her hand over the cream velvet cape.

"It has faux fur and look." I spun it around. "A hood."

"Very queen of the north," Margaret remarked. When we both stared, she clarified, *"Game of Thrones."*

"I love it," Vicki said. "That's you now, Jules. You're the queen of the north. Donovan Sherman's queen."

"It even has inside pockets," I said, showing off the satin lining.

"Who was working the consignment shop?" Margaret asked. "Was it Sally?"

I shrugged. "I don't remember her telling me her name. Nice lady with light hair. I'd seen her before at the coffee shop."

Margaret shook her head. "Not Sally. Well, whoever she was, she sure hooked you up."

"She did." Hugging the soft cape, I stared at my friends, old and new. "Thank you for being here, both of you. I can't tell you how right this feels."

"How do you want your hair?" Margaret asked.

The three of us talked about options as we carried the dress and cape and made our way back to the master bedroom suite.

"Wait," Margaret said as we entered. "Will Donovan be coming in here to get ready?"

"No," I answered. "He has strict instructions, and his suit is ready for him downstairs."

Margaret turned the lock on the suite door. "Good. Let's get the two of you ready. There's a wedding this afternoon."

Vicki reached for my hands. "I love how happy you look."

"I feel happy. I don't have another word for it. I feel like this is how someone should feel on their wedding day."

While I didn't have my mother's aesthetician present, I had been doing my own hair and makeup since I was a preteen. With the number of party preparations and pretend makeup sessions Vicki and I had shared, we were more than capable at helping one another out. It didn't take too long to be staring back at our made-up reflections in the master bathroom mirror.

Vicki grinned as she sprayed hairspray over my hairdo. "Do you have a veil?"

"No, but in the garment bag that had the cape there's a box. The woman from the boutique brought it down to me as I was checking out at the consignment shop. It's a headpiece, and I think it will match perfectly.

"I'll go get it," Margaret volunteered.

When she came back to the bathroom, she had the box.

I prized the lid off and pushed back the tissue paper. "Look," I said as I lifted the rhinestone and pearl accessory.

"That will look perfect."

"There's another box in here," Margaret said, lifting a slender jewelry box.

"That's weird. The woman only told me about the headpiece." I took the box.

"Maybe Donovan snuck it in there?" Margaret suggested.

"I hope not. I wanted it to all be a surprise." I opened the top of the box and my stomach twisted. "It's pearls."

Vicki's eyes grew wide. "Phillip sent you pearls that day in Chicago."

I nodded as I lifted the string. "These aren't the same ones. I left those on the vanity in my old bedroom."

Vicki took them from me and held them up. "I mean, they're pearls. I can't say they're much different."

"Put them back," I said. "I don't need to wear a necklace." I feigned a smile. "Simple. Remember."

"My turn," Vicki said as she slipped into the dress Margaret brought.

It fit perfectly. The cut was simple and the color was a soft shade of jade green. Calf-length with long sleeves, I couldn't have chosen anything better.

"Did you hear the doorbell?" Margaret said, looking at her watch. "I bet Albert is ready for our transport."

"I need a few more minutes," I said as I touched up my lipstick.

"You're beautiful, Julia," she said.

"I concur," Vicki added.

"I'll let him know we're almost ready," Margaret said, slipping away.

"Don't let those pearls freak you out," Vicki offered. "I mean, the lady was probably just being nice."

"Yeah. The people here are so helpful."

A few minutes later, Margaret returned, carrying a bottle of champagne and three glasses. "I found this in the kitchen with a note from your husband-to-be."

My smile returned as I read the note.

A dream come true.

"He didn't sign it," Vicki said, peering over my shoulder.

"I think he knows we'll know it's him."

Margaret lifted the glasses. "Should I pour, or do you want to save it for later?"

"I think we'll have plenty of celebrating later," I said, "Let's have a prewedding toast."

"I'm in," Vicki and Margaret both agreed.

Chapter 33

Van

Wearing my suit with our marriage license in the breast pocket of my suit coat, I went to the front door. "Are you ready for the ladies?" I asked Albert.

He lifted a large manila envelope. "Yes. This came special delivery to the front gate. The driver wanted to be sure you had it before the wedding."

I took the envelope. "Before the wedding?"

I turned it over, looking for a name. "Did they say who it's from?"

Albert shook his head. "I'm sorry. The delivery woman didn't offer, and I didn't ask."

My thoughts were on the wedding. "Have you heard from Jonathon?"

"Yes. He's on his way to the cabin with Judge Nichols."

I reached for my topcoat. "I'll head over there. It's getting close, and I'm not supposed to see Julia in her dress."

Albert smiled. "Traditions."

Traditions and normalities.

They were new, and as I donned my overcoat, I decided I liked them. I could do this. I could be normal.

Taking the envelope, I made my way through the kitchen and through the breezeway out into the garages. Julia had planned the wedding at the cabin. I'd planned a small get-together at the house for afterward. I'd invited a few more people such as Connie and her husband, Eric. Vicki and I discussed Julia's parents and came to the decision that the call was Julia's. She'd said she would inform them later. That was fine with me.

The wedding and later celebration would be small. I'd given Connie instructions to deliver more food and drinks for later. It wasn't fair to ask Mrs. Mayhand to make everything. With a code to get through the front gate, Connie would be ready for us once the wedding was over.

My thoughts were on our celebration much later, the one up in our suite. Yes, Julia and I had a visitor spending the night, but it was our wedding night. I didn't plan to let it pass without our own private festivity. As I got into the truck, I remembered one piece of our wedding I'd forgotten.

Our wedding rings.

Luckily, I was ahead of schedule.

Sneaking back into the kitchen, I stopped, not wanting to run into Julia. Listening for voices, I hurried to my office. The rings were in their box in the top drawer of my desk. Slipping the box into my suit coat pocket, I paused back at the staircase.

This was finally it.

The door to the breezeway hadn't shut all the way. Going back out, I made sure it latched. Back in the truck, I waved at Albert as I drove down the lane out onto the public road before turning up the unusually well-traveled lane. Hell, the cabin could go months without a visitor and today it would practically be Grand Central Station. As I turned up the lane, my cell phone buzzed. Once I was at the cabin, I wouldn't be able to answer.

Pulling to the side of the lane, I put the truck in park as the name came up on my dashboard.

My head shook.

Of course, Lena would make it known she wasn't invited. I hit the green button ready to make my excuse. "I'll make it up to you."

"Jesus, Van. How did you know?"

"Know what?"

"What are you making up to me?" she asked. "Wait, first I have to tell you what is happening."

My gaze went to the clock on my dashboard. "Can this wait? I can call you back."

"Van, she isn't here."

"Who?"

"Madison," Lena said. "I should have known something was going on."

"What are you saying?"

"I told you that Phillip wouldn't allow me to visit in the last year. I hadn't tried until now. I was getting the runaround. I just met with the director of the facility here in San Antonio. She'd been on vacation and no one else would meet with me. Phillip took my name off all her documents."

"What are you saying?"

"I'm saying that Madison checked herself out over a month ago."

"How did she do that?"

"All I know is she's been out. I talked to Olivia. She didn't know. No one has tried to contact Brooklyn."

"What do you mean *no one?*" I asked. "My PI said Phillip was back in San Antonio."

"I'm on my way to Olivia's house, but I'm telling you that according to Olivia, Madison and Phillip are both MIA."

I suddenly recalled the envelope Albert had given me. Reaching for it on the seat to my side, I ripped the flap open. A handwritten note was attached to documents.

Holding my breath, I began to read.

Van,

You told me if I ever needed another favor to first give you my divorce papers. Here they are. I need your help. I'm not crazy. Once Phillip learns I've left the facility, he will be coming after me and you.

He's the one who needs to be stopped. Don't go through with the wedding. You were right. We belong together, for us and Brooklyn.

I need you, Van.

I'm waiting.

Madison

"Van, are you still there?" Lena's voice called through the truck speakers.

Fuck.

Attached to the note were divorce papers signed by Madison. Phillip's place of signature was empty.

"Van," Lena said again.

"She's here. I just opened an envelope that was delivered to the front gate. Lena, Madison is here."

"Where?"

I recalled Michael's information on the DNA. "She was staying in the old cabin."

"Is she still there?"

"Shit, no. I had it reinforced. Julia and I are marrying there in a few minutes."

"Where could she be?"

My mind searched for answers. The guesthouse was now occupied by Michael and Albert. The house where she'd stayed the last time she came to me was gone, a Christmas tree farm now.

Fuck.

I'd forgotten about a promise I'd made to her years

ago. I'd given her the answer on where to go. If she were on the property, there was only one option.

I put the truck in gear and turned the wheel. "I have to go, Lena. I need to call my security."

"Van, where do you think she is?"

My heart pounded against my breastbone. "In the house with Julia."

"Shit. Hurry."

I hit the disconnect button and called Julia's cell phone. It went immediately to voicemail. My tires screeched as I accelerated on the main road. Trees whizzed by as I passed other cars as if they were standing still.

I called Albert's number.

My breath caught as he answered. "Albert, is Ms. McGrath okay?"

"She's upstairs. Margaret said they needed a few more minutes."

"Go up there. I'm on my way."

"Your brother?" Albert asked.

"No, his wife. His ex-wife. Fuck, it's a woman."

Chapter 34

Julia

The cape slipped from my fingertips as I blinked. The room around me wobbled, much like the illusion of heat on hot pavement. The temperature began to rise.

Margaret slouched down on the sofa.

"Margaret?" Her name from my lips sounded odd. "Vicki," I yelled her name as her glass of champagne shattered on the edge of the hearth and she reached for the mantel.

"Don't drink it..." she mumbled as her knees buckled.

I'd only had a sip of the champagne, not as much as either of the other ladies. Yet my hands began to tremble as I tried to steady myself.

"You aren't wearing the pearls."

I turned to the unfamiliar voice. Blinking, I tried to focus. "W-what are you doing here?"

It was the woman from the consignment shop, the same one at the coffee shop.

The dress she wore matched mine.

The exact same.

In her grasp, she was holding the box with the pearls. "Let me help you."

I pushed my way past her to the bathroom. Turning on the faucet, I splashed water to my lips.

The light-haired woman came around the corner. "You're very pretty. Of course, you do have youth...that will fade."

My stomach cramped as I leaned forward. "Please leave."

My thoughts went to my phone, but I couldn't recall where I'd put it. "My bodyguard...."

"Oh, I think it's time for you to rest, Julia."

"No. My wedding."

She had my champagne flute. "Here. Take another drink."

I shook my head, swiping the flute from her grasp. The crystal exploded upon impact. Shards of glass and liquid littered the floor. "Vicki." I tried to scream, but my voice was merely a whisper. My fingers blanched as I held tight to the vanity. "I...I."

The woman smiled as my knees gave out and the cramping increased.

On my knees, I could see her lips moving and hear her voice, but everything around me was too far away —as if I were watching through a telescope. I flinched as she leaned down, pulling the hairpiece from my hair.

From my place on the floor, I watched as she added

the accessory to her hair. "I need to hurry. It's my wedding day."

"Who...?" I wasn't sure if the word was audible. "Who are you?"

Her smile faded as she adjusted a necklace with a large solitary diamond in the reflection. "You know who I am."

I shook my head. The pieces weren't falling into place.

"I'm the woman Van loves, the only one he's ever loved."

Her smile reminded me of a cartoon—too large and too exaggerated.

This woman wasn't real. She was a caricature in my mind.

"Van..." I could barely form the word. Everything was losing focus. "You're...?"

"You know who I am," she said again. "I'm Madison."

* * *

Thank you for continuing Van and Julia's journey. More twists and turns and sexy times are coming with the conclusion to the Sin Series, *BLACK KNIGHT*.

If you enjoyed the Sin Series, you could also check out

the recently completed DEVIL'S Series Duet, beginning with the free prequel "Fate's Demand" and book one *DEVIL'S DEAL* and Aleatha's dangerous mafia stand-alone romance *KINGDOM COME*.

Turn back to *Books by Aleatha* for a complete and up-to-date listing of all the stories Aleatha has to offer.

WHAT TO DO NOW

LEND IT: Did you enjoy *GOLD LUST*? Do you have a friend who'd enjoy *GOLD LUST*? *GOLD LUST* may be lent one time. Sharing is caring!

RECOMMEND IT: Do you have multiple friends who'd enjoy my dark romance with twists and turns and an all new sexy and infuriating anti-hero? Tell them about it! Call, text, post, tweet...your recommendation is the nicest gift you can give to an author!

REVIEW IT: Tell the world. Please go to the retailer where you purchased this book, as well as Goodreads, and write a review. Please share your thoughts about *GOLD LUST* on:

*Amazon, *GOLD LUST* Customer Reviews

*Barnes & Noble, *GOLD LUST,* Customer Reviews

*iBooks, *GOLD LUST* Customer Reviews

* BookBub, *GOLD LUST* Customer Reviews

*Goodreads.com/Aleatha Romig

Books by ALEATHA

SIN SERIES:

WHITE RIBBON

August 2021

RED SIN

October 2021

GREEN ENVY

January 2022

GOLD LUST

April 2022

BLACK KNIGHT

June 2022

UNDERWORLD KINGS:

KINGDOM COME

Stand-alone romantic suspense

DEVIL'S SERIES (Duet):

Prequel: "FATES DEMAND"

Prequel - March 18

DEVIL'S DEAL

May 2021

ANGEL'S PROMISE

June 2021

WEB OF SIN:

SECRETS

October 2018

LIES

December 2018

PROMISES

January 2019

TANGLED WEB:

TWISTED

May 2019

OBSESSED

July 2019

BOUND

August 2019

WEB OF DESIRE:

SPARK

Jan. 14, 2020

FLAME

February 25, 2020

ASHES

April 7, 2020

DANGEROUS WEB:

Prequel: "Danger's First Kiss"

DUSK

November 2020

DARK

January 2021

DAWN

February 2021

* * *

THE INFIDELITY SERIES:

BETRAYAL

Book #1

October 2015

CUNNING

Book #2

January 2016

DECEPTION

Book #3

May 2016

ENTRAPMENT

Book #4

September 2016

FIDELITY

Book #5

January 2017

* * *

THE CONSEQUENCES SERIES:

CONSEQUENCES

(Book #1)

August 2011

TRUTH

(Book #2)

October 2012

CONVICTED

(Book #3)

October 2013

REVEALED

(Book #4)

Previously titled: Behind His Eyes Convicted: The Missing Years

June 2014

BEYOND THE CONSEQUENCES

(Book #5)

January 2015

RIPPLES (Consequences stand-alone)

October 2017

CONSEQUENCES COMPANION READS:

BEHIND HIS EYES-CONSEQUENCES

January 2014

BEHIND HIS EYES-TRUTH

March 2014

* * *

STAND ALONE MAFIA THRILLER:

PRICE OF HONOR

Available Now

* * *

THE LIGHT DUET:

Published through Thomas and Mercer Amazon exclusive

INTO THE LIGHT

June 2016

AWAY FROM THE DARK

October 2016

* * *

TALES FROM THE DARK SIDE SERIES:

INSIDIOUS

(All books in this series are stand-alone erotic thrillers)

Released October 2014

* * *

ALEATHA'S LIGHTER ONES:

PLUS ONE

Stand-alone fun, sexy romance

May 2017

ANOTHER ONE

Stand-alone fun, sexy romance

May 2018

ONE NIGHT

Stand-alone, sexy contemporary romance

September 2017

A SECRET ONE

April 2018

MY ALWAYS ONE

Stand-one, sexy friends to lovers contemporary romance

July 2021

* * *

INDULGENCE SERIES:

UNEXPECTED

August 2018

UNCONVENTIONAL

January 2018

UNFORGETTABLE

October 2019

UNDENIABLE

August 2020

ABOUT THE AUTHOR

ALEATHA ROMIG

Aleatha Romig is a New York Times, Wall Street Journal, and USA Today bestselling author who lives in Indiana, USA. She grew up in Mishawaka, graduated from Indiana University, and is currently living south of Indianapolis as well as part of the year in Bradenton, Florida, USA. Before she became a full-time author, she worked days as a dental hygienist and spent her nights writing. Now, when she's not imagining mind-blowing twists and turns, she likes to spend her time with her friends and family, including her beloved grandchildren.

Aleatha released her first novel, CONSEQUENCES, in August of 2011. CONSEQUENCES became a best-selling series with five novels and two companions released from 2011 through 2015. The compelling and epic story of Anthony and Claire Rawlings has graced more than half a million e-readers. Her next series, INFIDELITY (not about cheating) hit New York Times, Wall Street Journal, and USA Today best-seller lists. Aleatha has since released over thirty-five novels in multiple genres: dark romance, romantic suspense, thriller, and romantic comedy. She went back to her dark roots with the new trilogies of the Sparrow Webs: WEB OF SIN, TANGLED WEB, WEB OF DESIRE, and DANGEROUS WEB and the Devil's Series Duet: DEVIL'S DEAL and ANGEL'S PROMISE.

The titles keep coming. Be sure to check out her website to stay up to date.

Aleatha is a "Published Author's Network" member of the Romance Writers of America, NINC, and PEN America. She is represented by Kevan Lyon of Marsal Lyon Literary Agency and Wildfire Marketing.

Stay connected. Sign up for her newsletter and follow here:

Facebook / Twitter / TikTok / Instagram / Pinterest / Bookbub

9 781956 414332